A TRUTH
OCCASIONALLY
ACKNOWLEDGED

A Truth Occasionally Acknowledged

A Jane Austen Novella

KATE SUSONG

 REVERTED PRESS

ISBN: 979-8-9938633-1-3
Reverted Press: Atlanta, GA

DEDICATION

To my Mr. Darcy

INTRODUCTION

It was my husband's idea in the first place. "Why don't we put those English literature degrees to work," he said. So Fitzwilliam and Elizabeth Darcy found themselves at a Georgia Tech tailgate, and I published the stories on my Substack, katesusong.com.

My mother enabled the madness by proofreading all 10 vignettes on Substack – and then my friend Leslie Owens kindly took the time to proofread the manuscript. I changed a few things again after that, so any mistakes have to be credited to me. I pressed my daughter into service – she doesn't like romance but read it all and said it was fine – but my son didn't help *at all*. Like applying to college is that time consuming.

To my readers on Substack: You've read what I've written and have told me to write more – a delightful compliment. Thank you for the encouragement.

Finally, an explanation would be incomplete without acknowledging Jane Austen's 250th birthday on December 16, 2025. Her novels continue to provide timeless material for page, stage, and screen because she saw through our brokenness and had hope in the promised happy ending. *Deus ex libris*.

CAST OF CHARACTERS
And the Novels Whence They Came
(Not in order of appearance)

Pride and Prejudice
Fitzwilliam & Elizabeth Darcy, *need no explanation*
Charles & Jane Bingley, *friend and sister to above*
Mary Bennet, *sister to Elizabeth and Jane*
Lydia Bennet-Wickham, *another sister to above*
George Wickham, *terrible husband of Lydia Bennet*
Catherine DeBourgh, *aunt to Mr. Darcy*
Anne DeBourgh, *daughter of Catherine DeBourgh*

Emma
Emma Knightly, *matchmaker*
Ms. Hetty Bates, *elderly friend of Emma's*
Augusta Elton, *self-important woman*

Mansfield Park
Tom Bertram, *eldest son and an alcoholic*
Edmund Bertram, *pastor and brother to Tom*
Fanny Price Bertram, *author married to Edmund*
Maria Bertram, *divorcée, sister to Tom and Edmund*
Henry Crawford, *actor and womanizer*
Mary Crawford, *concert harpist*
Mrs. Norris, *aunt to the Bertrams*

Persuasion
Walter Elliot, *elderly, arrogant man with dementia*
Anne Wentworth, *married daughter of Walter Elliot*

Sense and Sensibility
Mrs. Henry Dashwood, *mother of three women*
Elinor Dashwood-Ferras, *eldest daughter of Mrs. D*
Edward Ferras, *pastor, married to Elinor*
Marianne Brandon, *second daughter of Mrs. D*
Chris Brandon, *married to Marianne*
Meg Dashwood, *youngest daughter of Mrs. D*
John Willoughby, *charmer*

Northanger Abbey
Zach Morland, *one of the younger Morland brothers*
James Morland, *one of the elder Morland brothers*
Isabella Thorpe, *beauty queen and serial wife*

TABLE OF CONTENTS

Vignette 1

TAILGATING MR. DARCY

In which Darcy functions without Elizabeth for five minutes

"Elizabeth, don't wander off when we get there. When you see someone you know, just smile at them. Stand beside me, and let them come to you."

Elizabeth paused on the sidewalk milling with football fans and took her husband's hand.

"Will," she said with gravitas, "you sound like a profound snob when you say that. I mean, of course, you *are* a snob – but it's important, nevertheless, to pretend that you're not."

His lips clamped shut.

"That's right. There's nothing to say because it's true." She smiled and his expression melted. "Remember the old trick: if you don't know what to say, ask people about themselves. Everyone loves to talk about themselves.

Everyone except you," she amended, interlacing her fingers with his and pulling him up the sidewalk. "Is God a Georgia fan or a Georgia Tech fan..." she mused as the red and yellow leaves floated down like confetti outside Georgia Tech's Bobby Dodd Stadium in Atlanta.

"Clearly a Georgia fan," Will said with bitterness.

"The Saturday-after-Thanksgiving rivalry game is the most pitiable time of the year to be a Tech fan. I commiserate with you."

"You never know who will win until the game is played."

"Yes, you do."

They approached the large party tent on the Tower Lawn adjacent to the stadium where other scholarship donors had queued to receive their name tags.

"Why do we never go to a real tailgate, Elizabeth? *Gold and White Tailgate*," he read on the banner over the entrance, "and not a truck in sight."

"Take comfort that plenty of people will tail you, sweetheart. And here's the first one," she said.

"Fitzwilliam and Elizabeth Darcy, what a surprise!" said an elderly man's voice ahead of them.

"Do not leave me," breathed Will.

"Mr. Elliot! How nice to see you. How are you enjoying your new home at Canterbury Court?" Elizabeth said as she attached her name tag to her mutton-sleeved jacket and arranged Will's on his blazer lapel.

"Oh, I wouldn't call it my *home*," Walter Elliot said with a wheeze and a dismissive wave. "Just a short stay while I'm in poor health. I needed some extra help, and the doctor thought it would be best for me to move into one of those... those... 'senior living communities,' I believe they're called. It's only temporary. I'll be back in our neighborhood as soon as my health has returned."

"Oh! I thought your home had been purchased by someone else. Have I misunderstood?"

"Yes, entirely! I believe my people have found someone to take the estate for a short time until my return. They're nobody. No one you need to meet."

"We have met them several times walking the dogs, and they seem like friendly, down-to-earth people," Elizabeth said as they all moved under the tent with Mr. Elliot following Will closely.

"Yes, that's exactly what I'd call them – 'down-to-earth.' Oh, that's good. Very good," he chuckled as if she had uttered some incisive subtlety understood only by them. Darcy directed a penetrating look at Elizabeth to end the conversation.

"Well, my parents love their community at Canterbury Court and said that you're a... an interesting addition to it."

Will's eyebrows peaked.

"Oh, that's right. I forgot your parents lived there, Elizabeth," Mr. Elliot said as if smelling something unpleasant. "Well, that's good for them, I'm sure." Mr. Elliot turned to Will, leaving Elizabeth in barely contained laughter. "Tell me, Fitzwilliam..."

"Lizzieeeeee!" crooned a woman from the bar, and Elizabeth turned to find the beautiful Isabella Thorpe gliding towards her.

"Izzieeeeee..." Elizabeth said in her best imitation of their old college greeting, masking her amazement that 33-year-old Isabella would attend an outdoor fundraising party in November dressed more like a Hooters waitress than the beauty queen she was.

Isabella sidled up to her, hugging her arm and walking away with her as if in a three-legged race. "You must introduce me to Tom Bertram. He's here! Mansfield Industries – you know!"

"I know Tom Bertram..." Will heard Elizabeth say as she looked at him over her shoulder before disappearing into the crowd.

"What do you say, Fitzwilliam. Is it a good investment?" Mr. Elliot was saying, refusing to leave and tout his importance elsewhere.

"Hello, Darcy," said a familiar woman's voice on his other side.

"Hello, Caro. Do you know Walter Elliot? Mr. Elliot, this is Caroline Bingley, sister of my closest friend. Does this mean Charles is here, Caro?"

"That's all that I am, Mr. Elliot. The harbinger of my brother Charles. Yes, he's here. Where do you live in Atlanta, Mr. Elliot?"

"Well, my home is in Tuxedo Park, but just now I reside..."

"Darcy! Can you believe this weather? It couldn't be more perfect for the game. Have you gotten a drink yet? No, I see you haven't. Let me get you one."

"Don't leave me, Charles," Darcy said under his breath, shaking his friend's hand and nodding fraternally at his sister-in-law Jane.

"How could Lizzie have abandoned you? You hate these things," Elizabeth's sister Jane said, scanning the crowd for her.

"She was carried off by Isabella Thorpe in that direction," he indicated.

"Oh, dear. Who is Izzie trying to meet this time?"

"Tom Bertram."

"Oh no. Poor Tom. We can't. I'll go find them." Off she went.

"Thank you, Jane." To Charles he said, "Isabella's goods were attractively displayed as usual today."

"Sorry I missed that. I love window shopping, but when is she going to wake up? After two affairs and two failed marriages, can't she see that nobody wants his wife's... goods... on display like she's available for everyone? 'On sale! Buy one, get one free!' Did I get lost in that metaphor? Are we still talking about b–"

"It's a truth universally acknowledged that any single man in possession of a grain of sense does not want a wife who'll cost him a fortune in divorce lawyers."

"Well said. That's what I meant."

"Mr. Darcy, I knew I'd find you!" An eager twenty-something young man with dark curls approached, looking vaguely familiar.

I used to be an independent man, Darcy thought to himself. *How did I manage all of this without Elizabeth?*

"I'm sorry," he said. "Please remind me of your name."

"No, sir, we've never met before. But you know my sister Catherine. I'm Zach Morland."

"Ah. I thought I recognized you. You look just like her."

"Yes, people always say so. I wonder if I could ask you about a fundraiser I'm doing for my fraternity..."

"Certainly." Darcy took a card from his wallet and handed it to Zach. "Call the Foundation at that number and tell my secretary you spoke to me at the... the tailgate," he said with disappointment. "Make an appointment to see me. You can tell me about it there."

Zach's face shone. "Thank you, Mr. Darcy! I knew you'd come through. Catherine always said you were really generous."

"Oh. That's... It's nothing... How did you get into this party?"

"I snuck in the back through the bushes! One of my pledge brothers bet me fifty bucks that I wouldn't get to talk to you, but now I have your card to prove it! I'll call you, Mr. Darcy, thanks!"

"He really does look like Catherine," Charles said.

"Oh? Did that occur to you before? You can be helpful any time, you know. Where is Elizabeth?"

"Mr. Darcy, what a pleasure to see you again!" Augusta Elton wormed through the crowd with her husband in tow. The profusion of ruffles on her blouse captured Darcy's attention.

"Augusta Elton," Charles murmured.

"Mrs. Elton, how are you?" Darcy said, shaking one of her extended hands to forestall an embrace.

"You have the most extraordinary memory for names, Mr. Darcy. You must meet hundreds of people, every one of them asking you for money, and yet you still care about the little people."

As the Eltons were somewhat short, Darcy wondered if the joke were intentional and decided not.

Charles showed his worth again. "Mrs. Elton, I believe the last time we saw you was at the Atlanta Opera Gala. Do you also take an interest in football?"

"I'm sorry; I didn't catch your name, young man."

"Excuse me – my closest friend, Charles Bingley," Darcy said, glancing around for Elizabeth.

"Oh! Any friend of yours must be... You were at the Opera Gala, you said? I don't recall seeing you there. Perhaps your table was further back?"

"Darcy! Give me a call and let's play a round. We'll meet out at the country club!" A convivial man with fat fingers passed a card over Mrs. Elton's shoulder. She recoiled as if the man were diseased and looked for sympathy from Darcy who took the card and began to look for the exits.

"Mrs. Elton, I didn't know you were interested in football!" Elizabeth swept back into the circle, and Darcy's shoulders relaxed. She handed him a flute of champagne, and he winced as if to say, *At a tailgate?* She shrugged and continued. "My sister Jane enjoyed working with you on the last Decorator's Showhouse. You really saved the day with your eye for flower arranging."

"Oh, did she say that? How perceptive of her."

"Mr. and Mrs. Darcy, if you'll turn this way. Smile, and..." A shutter clicked. "Thank you!"

"Mr. Darcy, it's about time to head to your seats. If you'll follow me, we have you seated in the President's Box..." An intern bobbed close by.

"Thank you, but I'd like to use my own tickets and just sit in the stands."

"Oh, sir!" The intern's voice became operatic. "The University President was particularly looking forward to hosting you this afternoon!"

"Before you go, Mr. Darcy," Mrs. Elton interrupted, "I'd like to ask you about my fundraiser for the Speech School. I hope you'll consent to being our guest speaker; your foundation has done such important work in mitigating the effects of –"

"Sir, I hope you'll come with me to sit with the President..." The intern visibly began to sweat as his one job threatened to implode.

"Of course, it would be an honor to sit with Dr. Cabrera," Elizabeth said with a wink at her husband. "We'll be right with you." Turning to Mrs. Elton, she said, "Mrs. Elton, what a flattering invitation. Could you please send me the date of your fundraiser, and we'll see if we're available?" Elizabeth handed her a card. "Please excuse us, we must run. Charles, try to rescue Jane. She's protecting Tom. See you at dinner." Turning to the grateful intern, she said, "Shall we?" as they left the tailgaters behind.

Vignette 2

WAIT

In which Tom Bertram sobers up.
Will Mary Crawford notice?

Tom Bertram left the tailgate needing a cold shower. He never should have accepted that invitation – it was too severe a test after rehab to deny himself that many proffered drinks. After surviving Thanksgiving that week, he'd thought he was ready, and he was wrong. Add the full frontal assault of Isabella Thorpe's cleavage, and decision fatigue had nearly finished him. Charles Bingley had seen his resolve fraying and adroitly introduced Isabella to another man eager to be shot down. Charles was a good friend. He wished he had what Charles and Jane had.

It was better that he hadn't stayed for the afternoon game anyway, he thought as he unlocked his Tesla and collapsed in the seat, leaning his head against the steering wheel. Tonight was the big night. He was going to speak to her. Hadn't he made it through that party without a drink? He sat up and looked out the windshield at the light glancing off the falling leaves. Maybe he had been ready for the tailgate, after all. He'd made it through successfully. Next time it wouldn't be so hard. He had passed through a long winter of his life, but now he was a new man. She would see that and give him a chance.

He shifted the gear and glided out of the garage, merging with traffic on North Avenue, listening to the diminishing sound of the college band playing their crashing fight songs in Bobby Dodd Stadium. Atlanta traffic was bearable on Saturdays.

He wondered where she was right then. How did she prepare for an evening performance? Did she rest in the afternoon? Who were the people who traveled with her and took care of things? Did she stay in a hotel when she performed in Atlanta? Or did her brother Henry put her up? Tom hadn't spoken to Henry in ten years – not since Henry had played fast and loose with all the women in Tom's family.

What will she wear tonight? he wondered as he showered. *Will she play an encore tonight?* he thought as he selected a spread collar shirt and tie. *Will she be available to talk afterwards?* he hoped as he made himself a club soda with grapefruit juice. He pulled a meal pre-made by his nutritionist from the fridge and ate it standing at the counter, knowing that this wouldn't change, that she wouldn't see him. What did he think was going to happen? That the world's leading concert harpist would suddenly give it all up to settle down with him? That he'd come home to find her cooking dinner and raising their kids?

He tossed the empty container in the trash and placed the fork in the dishwasher that held a week's worth of forks and glasses. Maybe he'd run it tonight. The housekeeper was coming tomorrow and would put the dishes away.

In spite of misgivings, Tom turned off the lights and continued with the plan. He drove south from his high rise condo on Peachtree Road, lights twinkling for Christmas, past his favorite wine store in the Peachtree Battle Shopping Center, past Piedmont Hospital where he'd spent the initial part of his rehab, over the bridge that spanned I-85 where he'd nearly jumped two years before, around the curve of Peachtree Street, and past First Presbyterian Church where he'd been baptized as an infant. He turned at the High Museum of Art where he'd spent many hours sketching the masters and joined the line of cars on 16th Street waiting to enter the parking garage.

The elevator opened onto the windy plaza between the white shining facade of the High Museum and the concrete Woodruff Arts Center where concert-goers scuttled through the swinging glass doors into the Christmas-swagged interior. Tom held the door for a group of women whose grateful smiles lingered in admiration of his impressive height.

One woman looked twice and said in a depressed voice, "Oh. Hi, Tom."

He peered at her and detected a familiar face under the thick glasses. One of Elizabeth Darcy's younger sisters. The unattractive, musical one. What was her name?

"Mary Bennet. How are you? You like the harp?"

"I am a pianist, as you know. The harp is essentially a piano standing on its end whose strings are plucked instead of struck with a felt hammer."

Tom prepared for a lecture as he held the second set of doors for her.

"I find Mary Crawford's adaptations of organ and piano music for the harp to be masterful. Have you ever heard her play Bach's Toccata and Fugue in D Minor?"

"In Berlin. She performed with the Berliner Philharmoniker and played that as an encore. It was extraordinary."

"You've seen her play it live?" A new respect for Tom dawned on Mary Bennet's pinched face. "I've only ever seen it on YouTube. Though I guess my view of her fingering was closer than yours from the audience." Mary regarded Tom curiously. "Did you know Mary Crawford growing up? I was too young to run in her circles, but you might have known her..."

"I did – we haven't kept in touch. She used to play pretty often for our family at home when we were younger. You might remember that she and her brother were orphaned as teenagers, and my parents sponsored them for a while."

Mary's face dropped as all the gossip she'd heard growing up returned to mind.

"Ah. You do remember," Tom said. "We do not keep in touch with her brother Henry."

"How is your sister Maria? And her – their – child?"

"Both are well, thank you. Eddie is ten years old now. Yes, named for my younger brother. I was not the hero of that story."

"And your brother Edmund and Fanny Price are..."

"Happily married and well, thank you. Ed pastors a church on the Westside, and Fanny writes comedic histories for children. They have two kids now."

They had reached the door of Symphony Hall and queued to show their tickets.

"Well, you've really turned your life around since those days," Mary said while locating her ticket on her phone.

This conversation had now exceeded the maximum politeness requirement for a friend's sister.

"Where are you sitting, Mary?" He glanced at her ticket. "Ah, I'm on the other side of the house. It was good seeing you. Enjoy the performance."

He stepped into the yawning Symphony Hall – formerly renowned for its terrible acoustics before installing its $500,000 acoustical shell courtesy of the Darcy Foundation – and moved down the left aisle toward the third row where he had selected his seat.

Early in his career of following Mary Crawford, he had learned that sitting right of center commanded an excellent view of a harpist's finger-work. But from that angle, Mary's hair fell over her face, so anyone in love with her would need to sit left of center.

He scooted past a dozen already-settled patrons as the lights dimmed and the cacophony of strings rehearsing, woodwinds squawking, and brass blasting arpeggios resolved itself into a single reedy note that the rest of the instruments matched in pitch. Following a silence, the conductor walked to center stage amid polite applause and bowed before taking the podium.

Music directors always did this: The soloist drew the crowd, but they saved her until the second half. The first half of the concert consisted of an orchestral piece Tom didn't care about followed by some contemporary composition to educate the audience that absolutely no one cared about. He began to plan his week as the pastoral melody of Dvorak's *American Suite* passed over him.

By the time he'd finished mentally writing the upcoming speech to his Board of Directors, the conductor had been applauded and resumed his position. Tom glanced at his program – this next piece was by someone named Julia Perry. At least she had died back in the 1970s, so this music might have stood the test of time. It was entitled *A Short Piece for Orchestra*. Well, it had that going for it. Tom waited with a modicum of hope for the opening notes – but his expectations were met with a noise from the stage that evoked a traffic jam. He returned to his speech.

The intermission, like a seventh inning stretch, allowed him to awaken a bit and remind himself why he didn't simply skip the first part of these events: purchasers of the cheap seats were descending en masse to the closer, empty seats they had noticed during the first half. The one time he'd arrived during intermission involved a tussle for his seat with an elderly woman, an experience he would never willingly repeat.

The stage crew rolled Mary's harp onto the stage and placed it left of the podium. The lights dipped in the signal that his life was about to resume. After the conductor, Mary would take the stage and be seated a few yards from him, her vivacity filling the room. The silence stretched Tom's nerves as he waited for her to appear.

The clicking of her heels offstage heralded her entrance, met by enthusiastic shouts, drumming of feet, and wild applause as she strode to her instrument. Her gauzy black gown flowed around her, and she curtsied deeply to the audience.

Tom sat transfixed by her beauty as she arranged the swaths of her dress and stretched her fingers across the strings. She nodded to the conductor, and Reinholt Glière's *Concerto for Harp and Orchestra in E Flat Major* began as if mid-kiss in a schmaltzy 1940s love scene. The music flowed through Mary's fingers, and the passion on her face reflected the urgency of the arpeggios as they reached higher in ever-increasing climaxes. Resplendent, transcendent, magnificent. How could this woman whom he'd alienated with his drunkenness ever turn to him? When he spoke to her tonight, her expressive eyes would tell him if he had a chance: to stay or to leave – he would know.

Tom leaned in his seat and traveled with Mary over the landscape of the music, visiting every note and exploring every chord with her. He was no musician, but his fingers thrummed in response to the glissandos as her elegant hands flew over the strings. The final rush of notes culminating in the stately closing chords left the audience breathless before they leapt to their feet with shouts of "Brava!! Brava!!" – applauding, beating their programs on seats, crying in amazement at her virtuosity.

Four curtain calls later, Tom thought she looked tired, ready for it to end, and she didn't emerge for a fifth. Perhaps she would be too tired to see him, he thought, anticipating and outwitting disappointment. He filed out of his row with the other patrons and stood by the stage door in the hallway. This had to be timed right. He wanted to catch her before she left her dressing room but to wait until the halls had cleared of departing musicians. He didn't want their first conversation to be observed by the whole orchestra.

Tom allowed a pushy mother to take her little prodigies in front of him through the door where she glanced around and then headed down the stairs to the dressing rooms. About a dozen other intrepid souls followed her, and Tom brought up the rear, always looking like he belonged wherever he went in his navy suit and tie. He nodded to a few techies stacking chairs and sauntered down the steps.

Following the crowd, he saw a gathering outside Mary's dressing room and hung back, waiting to see what would happen. In all the years he had watched her perform in various concert halls all over the world, he had never done this, never tried to see her. He had waited until now – until he was sure he wouldn't let her down, wouldn't drink again when pressed, wouldn't get hooked by another woman who cast her lure his way. He knew he'd changed, but would she see it?

In a heart-stopping moment, Mary Crawford opened the door and stood facing her fans with a smile. Her chestnut curls surrounded her valentine face, paler than usual but peerless in its soft beauty. The children held up programs to be signed while their mothers pushed them forward. She posed for selfies and portraits, signed CDs, and scanned the hallway with tired eyes to see how many more minutes she would need to be there when her glance alighted on Tom standing apart from the group.

For a moment, she froze with recognition, and he looked back at her, waiting for her anger, her disgust, her annoyance. He didn't breathe until a slow smile spread across her face, her eyes glowing with delight. Tom's smile rivaled hers, and he chuckled with disbelief at this reception.

"Wait for me," she mouthed over the heads of her fans, watching for him to confirm.

He nodded with a smile. He could wait. He *would* wait.

Vignette 3

THE ONE

*In which Mary Crawford has it all…
but knows there's more*

E arlier that day, Mary Crawford had emerged refreshed from her nap at 3:00 p.m., ready for the sold-out, Saturday-after-Thanksgiving performance. She would arrive at Atlanta's Woodruff Arts Center around 6:30 to tune her harp and warm up her fingers. In the meantime, she wandered around her brother's loft apartment in her robe and slippers looking at their family photos and trying not to disturb Henry, who sat on the sofa reviewing his lines for an upcoming film.

She lingered over an early photo her parents had used as their Christmas card the year when Henry and she had been 17 and 15 years old, taken a week before the car accident that left them with trust funds for comfort. Her mom had made her wear that fuzzy sweater she hated.

The memory of that year felt like a pill lodged in her throat.

Most of Henry's pictures on his corkboard Wall of Fame featured his co-stars from various films and series, the famous people he'd met, and some blasts from the past. There were Elizabeth and Fitzwilliam Darcy at some gala or other. There were Anne and Fred Wentworth on that cruise that Henry had performed on. Oh, no, was Henry still hanging out with George Wickham? George could lead a brick wall astray. Not that Henry needed help. Wow, was that Meg Dashwood? She had really grown into a beauty. Who was...

"Hold on, is that Isabella Thorpe?" Mary blurted out. "Those can't be real. She wasn't that busty in high school."

"Spoken like a jealous woman," Henry said, turning a page.

"Real or not real?"

"How would I know?" Henry said, not looking up.

"Oh, please. Don't tell me you're the only man in Atlanta who hasn't –"

Mary stopped. She cocked her head, wincing like a note had sounded out of tune. "Bad habit – that's not me anymore," she said. "Sorry. I would've said that... many times in the past, but... I'm tired of that person."

She went back to looking at the pictures while Henry watched her.

After a considered silence, he said, "Something going on with you, Mary?" When she didn't respond, he said, "Whatever happened with you and Judd? You said you broke up a few months ago, but I kinda thought... that you thought he was the one."

"Hmmm," Mary said, still looking at the pictures. "The One. We're a generation of women looking for *The One*."

"Yeah, I love being that guy. For a night or two."

Turning around, she said, "The One who wants to get married but doesn't want me to quit my career or settle down. The One who will do everything 50-50: laundry, dishes, cleaning, diapers. The One who will never cheat on me but will never want me to have sex at inconvenient times. The Right One will also be tall and handsome and rich with the potential to be a good father with no emotional baggage. Know anyone like that, Henry?"

Henry snorted and went back to his script.

"No, it turns out no one else knows him either. Judd wasn't The One. Neither was Tim or Larry – or Dev or Scott."

"Or Abe."

Mary frowned. Certainly not Abe. "And after a decade of looking, I've started to realize that The One is a mythical beast whom, it turns out, no one has actually ever sighted." She sat down next to Henry on the sofa and whispered, "Oh, there are rumors of him." She gestured toward the Wall of Fame. "I sometimes think Charles Bingley or Fitz Darcy fits the description pretty well." She mused on those tall, handsome, rich men for a moment. "But then, you never know what goes on behind closed doors. Others seem to have found The One, but almost everyone ends up divorced."

"Biological clock ticking? You are 33."

"Shhhh. Shhhh. No, it's more like... rather than custom order the right man or complain that no one is good enough... I've decided that *I* want to be good enough."

"Because the world's leading concert harpist isn't already good enough?"

"No... no... I don't know. I can't explain." She looked at her brother as he studied his script. "There aren't any pictures of your son on that wall. How is he?"

There was a long pause before he said, "I don't know. I'm not allowed to see him."

The siblings sat in silence on the sofa listening to the sounds of traffic in Atlanta's Old Fourth Ward, the cavernous space of the converted warehouse yawning around them, increasing their isolation.

After several minutes, Mary broke the silence. "Do you ever think about the Bertrams?"

"Maria Bertram gave birth to my son. She crosses my mind once in a while."

"I mean Fanny and Edmund... What almost happened..."

Henry didn't respond.

"I got the sense... just tell me if you don't want to talk about it... but I got the sense at the time that Fanny would have been the right one for you – that everything would have turned out well and you both would have been happy... if –" The conclusion was too much for Mary to verbalize.

"If I'd been who I should've been."

Yes, Mary thought. She said aloud, "And I don't mean to say that you're the only one. I messed everything up with Edmund."

"You never would have been happy with Ed, Mary. You could not be a pastor's wife. I believe it helps to be a Christian."

"Right. I don't mean that I wish I'd married Ed. Definitely not. I mean... I'm always trying to mold men into a perfect fit for myself without any consideration of... of how... I don't know."

"Of how you need to change?"

"Yes."

Another silence.

"So that's what happened with Judd? You decided you needed to change?"

"I was trying to describe to him this sense that I wanted something more – more from him, certainly, but more from myself, too. And he laughed and said what we had was perfect. I was free to travel the world and pursue my career, and he was free to... to do whatever he does when I'm not around. I think it suited him perfectly.

"But I told him, I realized that wanting more from him would require me to sacrifice, too – that I would need to scale back my concert schedule – even be willing to give it all up if I wanted something more – if I wanted a family with a committed husband and children."

"What did he say?"

Mary faced Henry and said, "It was the turning point of my life. He laughed and said, 'If you want that, why are you with *me*?'"

"Wow."

"Yeah. I left and went to a hotel and thought about it all night. The next day, I met him for breakfast and thanked him for opening my eyes. I haven't seen him since."

Henry waited for the sequel. "So.... What's changed? You're still touring. You've been in thirty cities in the last six months. I don't see you slowing down."

"No, but I'm willing to. Ready to. I have a sense that something is about to happen." She wrapped her robe tighter around her. "Do you ever see *Tom* Bertram?"

"What? No, I don't see any of the Bertrams. I permanently scuttled that relationship."

"Well, I do."

"Do what? See Tom? Where?"

"All the time. All over the world."

Henry looked disgusted. "Are you about to tell me that his image is engraved on your heart or something nauseating like that?"

"No, I literally see him at least once a month all over the world."

"Where?"

"At my concerts. He sits to my right on the third row. Just once or twice a month. I never know when he'll be there or where in the world I'll see him."

"Well, how is he? I can't believe he's speaking to us!"

"He's not. He never speaks to me or tries to see me. Even after 10 years..."

"I'm sorry, hold on. He's pursuing you around the world and never speaks to you? He doesn't bring you flowers and take you to dinner afterwards? Isn't that what your fans always do?"

"Yes. No, he never does that. I don't think he's there for me. I think he travels a lot for business and loves the harp."

"That's ridiculous. This is a heterosexual man we're talking about. A man with some serious baggage, by the way. He's a raging alcoholic whose sister I impregnated, destroying her marriage and making her infamous. It doesn't sound to me like he's The One."

"Oh, you didn't destroy my chances all by yourself. Do you recall that I entered the Bertram household at 16 years of age, fully prepared to seduce the oldest son? I targeted him and valued him only for his earning potential."

"I don't see you as the long-suffering wife of an alcoholic. Good thing you changed your mind."

"Good thing I targeted Edmund instead? Let's not call anything that followed a good thing."

"Fine. What in the world makes you consider Tom Bertram now?"

"I've changed."

"But he's an alcoholic."

"And I guess always will be, but he's changed."

"You can tell that from the third row?"

"I can tell."

She unfolded herself and stood to stretch. "But it doesn't matter."

It was time to shower and get ready for the hair and makeup artist to arrive.

"It doesn't matter," she said again. "He doesn't want anything to do with us. And I'm not going to target him again – in search of The One."

She headed toward the bathroom and turned at the door. "Wouldn't it be nice if things worked out the way they might have if we hadn't screwed everything up?"

Henry looked past her with hollow eyes.

"But that's not how real life works," she said as she clicked on the bathroom light and closed the door.

Vignette 4

LIP SERVICE

*In which we learn
what Mrs. Dashwood really thinks*

Mrs. Henry Dashwood, widow and mother of three grown daughters, sat in church on the Sunday morning after Thanksgiving and knew she had gone from the sublime to the ridiculous. Confident that the intensity of emotion she felt directly correlated to the level of worship she achieved, she decided that the true worship service had occurred last night at Atlanta's Symphony Hall. Mary Crawford had a true gift on the harp and had stirred her soul. This "worship music," on the other hand, was about to induce a migraine. If a church service required ear plugs, what did that say about the preaching?

She stood between her youngest two daughters and surveyed her fellow congregants. There was an unseemly number of young people here, as if this were a party. The shortness of the dresses and depth of the necklines revealed their true purpose in coming; though, she supposed, church was probably the best place to look for a husband. Was anyone here concentrating on the worship? The men must find all these girls very distracting, she thought. She glanced at her son-in-law over her daughter's head. He was singing the praise song with his eyes on the words projected on the screen. Her daughter Marianne had found this church, and Chris Brandon followed wherever the wind blew her – Marianne and her wild spirit, always searching for new highs.

Drums. Why must there be drums in church? Such a primitive and disruptive instrument. She cast her eyes about again and was surprised to count a large number of minorities in the room – not that that had anything to do with drums, she thought quickly. Diversity in church had been a long time coming, and she was certainly in favor of it. Her large-mindedness in coming here warmed her with a virtuous glow and strengthened her certainty.

A few congregants expressed a tendency toward movement with the music that Mrs. Dashwood found disconcerting. A snapping of fingers to her right drew her attention, and she frowned at her youngest daughter Meg, 21 years old and home from college for Thanksgiving weekend, whose eyes were closed as she snapped and swayed to the beat. Those college campus ministries had turned a generation of Christians into hippies. She half expected someone to hold up a lighter next.

The praise music finally ended – though why these kinds of songs never resolved on the tonic (as if they threatened to continue indefinitely), she would never understand – and she sat down with relief. One thing she favored about these new, evangelical churches was the padded chairs. After spending a lifetime on a barely cushioned pew in her historic church, she knew when to be grateful.

However, there was something deadening about worshipping the Lord in a converted storage facility. She missed her church in Savannah, GA with its stained glass windows – dedicated and paid for by her husband's great-great-grandparents, their names prominently displayed on a brass plaque near the pew on which Dashwoods had sat for generations. She glanced up at the ceiling crisscrossed with poles holding stage lights and projectors and missed the nave of her church soaring over the well-dressed congregants, echoing with the perfectly rehearsed tones of the professional choir – nothing like these volunteer musicians with their electric (electric!) guitars (guitars!).

The pastor took the stage, and Mrs. Dashwood's face fell in disbelief. She had known Edmund Bertram as a boy – had known his parents – but she was wholly unprepared for the stunning man who stood before them. It seemed in bad taste for a pastor to be so handsome. No wonder the room was packed to overflowing. Thank goodness he was married, otherwise there'd be trouble, she thought, glancing at single-and-available Meg whose face reflected Ed's smile from the pulpit. Mrs. Dashwood's son-in-law Chris had met the pastor at Crossfit. Obviously.

She now remembered that story from eight or ten years ago – something about Rev. Ed Bertram almost marrying the harpist Mary Crawford and then... Oh, that's right! Ed's married sister got pregnant with Mary Crawford's brother's child and the whole thing fell apart. How could she have forgotten? She shook her head, remembering the months of discussion that disaster provided. Not gossip, of course – it was all true.

Ed read the Scripture with energy instead of solemnity, which smacked of irreverence, she thought, and – after a brief, conversational prayer – launched into the sermon. Many of the young people around her had their Bibles open on their laps and took notes, either directly in the Bible or in separate notebooks – as if they were in school. Did they think there would be a test later? She thought of her dead husband with discomfort and shifted on her padded chair. Were these the things that would facilitate entry into the hereafter? She had always heard it was serving the poor and the oppressed that made you right with God, not knowing every little thing the Bible said.

These Bible-heavy churches didn't care about the poor, she thought, repeating something she'd heard someone say, and flipped over the order of service to read the announcements. *Clean up the trash in the neighborhood park... Tutor neighboring kids in Grove*

Park (Oh, that was a very depressed neighborhood. She'd never been there.)... *Mow lawns for the elderly in the neighborhood... Buy Christmas presents for children in families with one or more incarcerated parents* (Good Lord!)... *Fill shoeboxes with presents for Operation Christmas Child... Learn how to be a respite caregiver for foster children so foster parents can have a break.* (She could tutor children after thirty years of teaching 4th grade....)

Realizing that the homily should have concluded by this time, she checked her watch and returned her attention to Ed, surprised not to detect any summary phrases or declension of tone to imply that the end was nigh. On the contrary, Ed Bertram continued to preach full-bore, and no one around her packed up their pens or closed their Bibles or gave any other sign that they expected an imminent finale; rather, Marianne and Meg were riveted and still taking notes. How was it possible for someone to preach endlessly on a few verses in II Peter, which was so obscure, she'd never even read it before?

Her other son-in-law – Rev. Ward Ferras, husband to her eldest daughter Elinor – would never presume to preach this long. One of the hallmarks of his church services was brevity. His church in downtown Atlanta, where hardly anyone lived anymore, was not very well attended – unless you counted the homeless sleeping in the pews. His was a very difficult job, which made this visit to Marianne's new church all the more awkward.

She was half afraid someone would see her here and report her betrayal to Elinor.

With a twinge of annoyance, she realized this incident would join the long list of examples of how she favored Marianne – which she didn't. It was her youngest child, Meg, who wanted to come here, and Mrs. Dashwood merely wished to be with her before she returned to college that afternoon. Elinor wouldn't see it that way, however, and would wonder why they couldn't all come to Ward's church and worship together as a family. Unable to admit her discomfort with the homeless, her dislike of the musty smell from unrepaired roof leaks, the arctic temperatures from dysfunctional radiators, and a general lack of inspiration in Ward Ferras' preaching, she couldn't articulate a single reason for not joining Elinor's church, thereby increasing the tension between them. The legendary impossibility of finding downtown parking was belied by the church's empty parking lot, so she fell back on the more defensible ground of politeness to her hosts. Living with Marianne and Chris (temporarily, of course – just until she found her own place) demanded the barest courtesy of attending their chosen church. If Elinor had a problem with their choice, she could take it up with Marianne. Mrs. Dashwood shuddered at the thought of that conversation.

She finally heard the words "Let's pray" ending the sermon and checked her watch. Forty-two minutes. Unbelievable. The congregation bowed their heads, and Mrs. Dashwood looked at her diamond ring on her hand in her lap. It needed cleaning. Even so, those stage lights caused a mesmerizing sparkle that changed color as she tilted her finger. Further down the row in front of her, a young man's head turned, watching her ring flash. She glanced at him and then looked again. That was one of the Morland boys. All those children looked so similar, you couldn't tell them apart and would know them anywhere. This one was 22 or 23 years old with the familial black curls. With hair that unkempt, he must still be a student somewhere.

She had stopped turning her ring, but the boy continued to stare. With eyebrows raised, she closed her eyes in demonstrative prayer to alert the Morland boy to his impiety, but when she peeked again, he was still gazing in her direction. Such insensibility she could not fathom until she realized with disgust that he was staring at Meg, head bowed and eyes closed beside her. She rolled her eyes and drew a deep breath. Are women subject to the male gaze even during prayer? Meg did look remarkably beautiful with her long lashes brushing her cheek and her *retroussé* nose over pink lips, she thought – gazing at her, too.

Mrs. Dashwood spent the rest of the service considering the young men she would be glad for Meg to marry and those from whom she'd carefully shielded her. *The body of Christ broken for you* became that boy who'd shattered an arm in high school showing off a skateboard flip for Meg. *The blood of Christ shed for you* mixed with memories of the cute boy Meg had liked who'd gone to West Point. He would have taken Meg

God-only-knew-where in the world – no, thank you. She stood for the final hymn and sang "Amazing Grace" from memory while imagining a strong, handsome, rich man who would love Meg with such passion that he'd give up anything to live for her. Only the best for Meg.

Ed Bertram gave the benediction, and Mrs. Dashwood watched the congregation raise their hands like satellites to receive it. When it was over, everyone began to mill around, greeting their friends, introducing themselves to newcomers. Meg and Marianne knew several people whom they went off to hug, and Mrs. Dashwood watched that Morland boy make his way to Meg – no lack of confidence there. Mrs. Dashwood stood with a pained expression on her face wondering how all these people could convey such joy while under assault from the praise band's postlude.

Ah, there was Ed Bertram. She must go over and tell him that she knew his parents and remembered him as a boy.

"Ed Bertram, *there* you are! You have grown into *such* a handsome man! And what an *amazing* sermon that was. You are a *wonderful* preacher! I can't *wait* to come again. You couldn't *keep* me away!"

Vignette 5

THE COLOR OF HOPE

*In which James Morland forgives
Isabella Thorpe*

The bell on the door clanged as Zach Morland bumped it open, his arms full of boxes from the delivery truck that had just pulled away.

"Late!" his brother Jim yelled from the back of the store.

"I've been here for 20 minutes unloading moss! – which is heavier than you'd think," Zach said, hoisting the first load onto the counter.

"You have to tell me when you get here, otherwise you're late!"

"Well, since time is relative to your frame of reference," Zach said with unassailable cheerfulness, heading back to the front steps for more, "let's agree that 20 minutes haggling with that delivery guy was equal to one minute of whatever it is you're doing – and that I'm on time."

"Alright, Einstein," Jim Morland said, emerging from the back. With his reading glasses perched on his nose, he seemed unaware of an errant sprig of baby's breath clinging to his graying, familial black curls. "But the next time it happens, I'm docking your pay," he said, pointing a red rose at him.

"What's with you today, Jimmy?" Zach said, stacking the second load on the first and staring at the baby's breath. Never chipper, his elder brother seemed particularly humorless today. "Are you arranging the flowers yourself? Where's Lydia?"

"You tell me! It's the first Monday after Thanksgiving, and she's already failing to turn over that new leaf she promised the last time this happened. I won't put up with my employees waltzing in at whatever time suits them! We have fifteen arrangements to do before noon, and I can't possibly do it all myself!"

Zach swatted the baby's breath out of Jim's hair and said, "Come on. I'll help." Zach led the way into the flower-arranging room, which Jim kept so meticulously organized that he'd cut a large pass-through into the shop so customers could watch the magic happen.

"I'm not familiar with your aesthetic talents," Jim said. "No, Zach, you unpack the moss and resupply my crate here. Put the rest in the humidifier. Get the showroom straight before 10:00 and manage the customers. You have class this afternoon back at Tech, right?"

"Yep! Tomorrow's the last day of classes, then Reading Period, exams, and Christmas break! I've already got it planned out —"

"Tell me later. Get going."

Zach laughed and headed back to the showroom, which was in perfect order apart from the moss. He refilled the crate and the humidifier, broke down the boxes and swept the floor, all while maintaining an uninterrupted flow of information.

"I know you want to hear the good news: I've met the girl I'm going to marry. Now, before you say anything — yes, she likes to play Pictionary. She's a junior at Auburn, so I'll have to wait a couple years, but that'll let me get established somewhere in my graduate program. I won't hear from CalTech or Harvard until the spring, but now that I've met her, I'm inclined to stay on the East Coast. Now wait for it, Jimmy: the *crème de la crème* is that I met her at church, which will win instant approval from Mom and Dad, don't you think?"

"Wait," Jim said, stepping into the showroom with a pair of shears and a fistful of calla lilies, "you met who?"

"Whom, Jimmy. I met her. The girl I'm going to marry. Meg Dashwood. Here's a picture of her." Zach pulled out his phone and presented the picture with a flourish. Jim flipped down his readers and examined the image.

"You took a picture of her while she was praying?"

"Yes. It would have been weird otherwise."

Jim glanced at Zach and back at the picture.

"She's beautiful. But as I can tell you from long experience, that is the least important and most fleeting thing about a woman. Find out if her character is beautiful first."

"It is. I talked with her. She radiates beauty like a star."

"Does she know yet that you're a budding astrophysicist?" Jimmy asked, getting back to work.

"Yes, I told her I'm going to be an astronaut, and she said, 'What, like a four-year-old?'"

Jimmy barked a laugh from the arranging-room. "I like her! Sounds like she'll keep you humble."

"Yeah, she's funny. I hope to get her to come to one of our family parties this Christmas."

"Why don't you have a date first? If you still like her, you can bring her here."

"And introduce her to the dragon first? I think I'll leave you for last, Jimmy."

"Just be careful, Zach."

"OK, Jim." Zach refrained from saying, *Not everyone is Isabella Thorpe, Jim. And not everyone is as gullible as you were.*

That wasn't fair, though. Hadn't Jim done exactly what Zach just had – fallen in love with a girl at first sight? Jim had believed no wrong of the magnificent Isabella Thorpe and had ignored every red flag until he caught her *in flagrante delicto* with his sister's brother-in-law right before the wedding. Their sister's holidays on that side were really awkward.

Zach had been in second grade when it happened, but he still remembered his older brother's grief and how it changed him. No longer sweet and hopeful, everything became doom and gloom with him. Fifteen years should be the statute of limitations on grudges, and that time had expired.

"Ten o'clock," Jim called. "Open up!"

It was actually 9:59, but Jimmy liked to catch everyone not doing their job. With a smile and a shake of his head, Zach put on his forest green apron with *Firwoods* embroidered on the bib and unlocked the front door.

There were two fit middle-aged women in yoga pants and heavy coats holding their coffees and chatting about their Thanksgiving weekend while another woman emerged from the warmth of her car when she saw the store open.

"Good morning, ladies!" Zach said with a smile, holding the door wide. "Let me know if I can help you with anything." They said good morning – they were just there to browse.

The woman from the car – young, in a snug pantsuit – marched up and said, "I'm here to pick up the order for the Darcy Foundation. The two large urns? I thought you opened at nine. I'll need help getting them to the car."

"Of course. I'll grab those for you."

Zach strode to the back and found the twin arrangements already stabilized in boxes for moving. As he carried the first one out, he passed Jimmy arranging moss over the dirt of an elegantly potted orchid.

"Lead the way," he said to the intern, her condensed breath puffing like a locomotive.

Both arrangements secured in the floor of the minivan, Zach jogged back inside, holding the door for three more shoppers and saying, "How may I help you, ladies?"

A magisterial older woman in a fur coat with elegantly coiffed, silver hair spoke, inclining her head toward the favored plants. "I want those poinsettias potted in this urn." She pronounced the word *pwan-SET-ee-uhs* and set a sterling silver trophy cup nearly the size of a punch bowl on the counter.

"Certainly," Zach said, removing the urn to the potting room and coming back for the poinsettias. "Is there anything I can help you with, ladies?" he said to a pretty woman in her early-thirties and her elderly companion.

"What did he say, Emma? I'm afraid my hearing aid isn't aiding me very much. Oh! Did you hear what I said? Hearing aid, aiding me? I didn't mean to say that, but it was funny." She chuckled at herself. "I don't seem to be able to understand him. Did you hear what he said?" The older woman leaned on her cane, shaking slightly, and cocked her head.

"Yes, Ms. Bates. He wants to know how he can help us." The younger woman smiled at Zach and continued, "But I think we'll just look around for a few minutes."

Taking the plants to the next room, Zach stood at the counter beside Jimmy, who had made great progress on the arrangements. Zach re-potted three pwan-SET-ee-uhs, pressed moss onto the dirt, and boxed the repurposed punch bowl while listening to the three shoppers.

The fur-coated lady said, "Did you see that woman just now at the coffee shop, Emma? The one in the high heels and hot pants that seemed to have been spray-painted onto her body? That was Isabella Thorpe."

Jimmy became very still beside Zach.

"You know, she won the Miss Georgia beauty pageant years ago but has not lived up to the standards expected of her."

Showing a chinoiserie pot to her elderly companion, Emma replied, "Who among us has, Mrs. DeBourgh?"

Mrs. DeBourgh looked as if *she* had, and said, "Emma Knightly, don't tell me that you are unaware of the scandals surrounding that woman. How can Atlanta's premier matchmaker protect her wealthy clients without knowing who the gold-diggers are?"

"You are right as always, Mrs. DeBourgh. I *do* know, but it's part of my job not to *discuss* it." Emma turned to the elderly lady. "What do you think of this pot, Ms. Bates? I want you to pick whichever one you think will look best in your living room."

"You are so kind, Emma. You always have been. So kind. I told your husband just the other day how kind you are. 'Mr. Knightly,' I said, 'Emma is so kind.' And what do you think he said? He said, 'You're right, Ms. Bates. Emma is kind.'"

"Well, I'm happy to have your confirmation that she *is* a gold-digger," continued Mrs. DeBourgh, ignoring

Hetty Bates and magnanimously overlooking Emma's rebuff. "Three times married and twice divorced – her last husband old enough to have been her grandfather and barely cold in his grave – and she's already on the hunt for the next one."

"I love this store," said Ms. Bates, blissfully deaf to the conversation. "The Morland family used to own it many years ago. Do they still?"

Emma glanced at Zach's black curls through the doorway as she said, "I believe so, Ms. Bates."

Mrs. DeBourgh declined to acknowledge the change of subject. "My own daughter Anne is Isabella Thorpe's age and, though a beauty in her own right, would never *dream* of dressing in the flagrantly immodest way favored by our *beauty queen*." She served the last words garnished with acid.

Checked by the depth of self-delusion that could describe Anne DeBourgh as a beauty, Emma could only reply, "I can understand your feelings on the subject. Oh, that's a pretty one, Ms. Bates." She pointed to the next table.

The old woman tottered toward a crystal bowl and said, "Jimmy Morland was such a sweet boy. I taught him in Sunday school twenty – no, thirty-five years ago!"

"Emma, I see you recall that my nephew Colonel Fitzwilliam succumbed to her wiles several years back," continued Mrs. DeBourgh, allowing her own train of thought full steam and making connections where none existed. "Thank God, I was able to put a stop to what would have been a *disastrous* marriage – though not everyone has paid attention to my wisdom..." She seemed to dwell with ire on an unforgotten instance in which someone had ignored her opinion.

"You are right that the Colonel and Izzie would not have been well suited – for several reasons, I think. Your other nephew and Elizabeth Bennet are very happy, though!" Emma said, recalling too late that Mrs. DeBourgh's well-known disapproval of that marriage stemmed from her failure to secure Fitzwilliam Darcy for her daughter Anne.

Mrs. DeBourgh gave her a look of deep offense.

Emma backpedaled. "Matters of the heart sometimes elude the wisest guidance," she said, throwing Mrs. DeBourgh a bone and leading her to more profitable thoughts. "I've always said that if you'd trust me with Anne, we'd find the right man for her in no time."

Mrs. DeBourgh stiffened.

"You have given her everything she needs to succeed in the world – and there are new ways for eligible men to see what a wonderful daughter you have. Don't forget you can call me any time to discuss."

"What do you think of this one, Emma?" Ms. Bates pointed to the smallest, least attractive pot in the shop.

"Oh, no, Ms. Bates. Not for your lovely coffee table. Keep looking."

"We do not flaunt our advantages as *some* do," Mrs. DeBourgh said, not finished with Isabella Thorpe. "*Izzie*, you call her? Don't tell me you're *friends* with that woman!"

"Isabella and I were in the same sorority at Vanderbilt – along with Elizabeth Bennet. I've been sorry to see the heartache Izzie has suffered over the years."

"Entirely self-inflicted!"

"So many of our problems are, don't you think, Mrs. DeBourgh?"

Ms. Bates lingered near the crystal bowl that had attracted her earlier and said in a quavering voice, "I recall that Jimmy Morland was engaged to marry that beautiful Thorpe girl many years ago. Now why did I think of her after all these years –"

"I think this one would look best, Ms. Bates – what do you think?" Emma said belatedly, diving for the crystal bowl.

"James Morland was engaged to Isa—? One of the Morland brood? Now *that* I did *not* know," Mrs. DeBourgh said. "Very interesting. I wonder why Isabella Thorpe thought to sell herself short."

Emma blushed and said, "Mrs. DeBourgh, I think you must have forgotten that this shop is owned by—"

"That'll be $226.94," Jim Morland said, appearing behind the cash register, his face flaming with humiliation. "Would you like to use a credit card?"

The front door swung open, knocking a small vase to the floor where it smashed.

"Sorry, sorry, sorry! I'm here, I'm here, I'll clean that up." Lydia Bennet-Wickham halted in front of Mrs. DeBourgh and saw expressions of fury and mortification ranged before her – with the exception of Ms. Bates, who seemed very pleased with her crystal pot.

"Oh!" Lydia burst out laughing at the perfect storm she had sailed into while Mrs. DeBourgh looked as if an unspeakable stench had wafted through the door.

"Just put it on my account and bill me," said Mrs. DeBourgh. "I must run to the Children's Hospital board meeting. Emma, give my regards to your husband. It was good to see you, Hetty. Carry that to my car for me, young man," she said to Zach, who had trailed Jimmy in a speechless daze, as she led the way out the door with the stateliness of a funeral march.

When Zach returned, Ms. Bates had chosen her pot and plant, which he took to the arranging room while straining to catch any conversation at the cash register.

Lydia scraped the glass into a dustpan while Emma Knightly said in a bright tone, "You have such a beautiful store here, Mr. Morland. It's one of my favorites – where I always buy gifts." She shuffled for her credit card and her words before saying barely audibly, "You may have overheard that I have a private matchmaking business. Any young lady would be lucky to meet a hardworking, successful, and handsome man like yourself. If you are interested, it would be my pleasure to give you a free consultation."

She paid for Ms. Bates' gift and carried it out herself, assisting Ms. Bates down the steps, leaving Zach to wonder if he should check on his brother in the showroom or start on the mammoth arrangement of roses for some lady's 90th birthday. Just as Zach nearly abandoned his post, Jim walked into the arranging room with multiple boxes of red roses, laid them on the counter, and began to remove the outer, wilted petals. Zach had seen many flowers take the ruthless brunt of Jimmy's temper, but unexpectedly, he pulled the damaged petals with care and examined the newly exposed beauty as if he'd never before seen a rose.

Zach observed this uncharacteristic operation and opened his mouth to say something (anything!) to dispel the overheard insults – when his eyes fell across a card lying on the counter between them. It was Emma Knightly's business card that Jimmy hadn't thrown away as he had discarded every previous attempt to set him up. Zach glanced at Jimmy – now *smelling* the rose – and back at the card. It read, "Emma Knightly, Matchmaker, Discreet and Personal Service" — and under her name hovered a heart, blood red, the color of hope.

Vignette 6

Resurgens

*In which Henry Crawford and
George Wickham meet for drinks*

T he lights were low as Henry Crawford stepped
into Atlanta's St. Regis Bar. He'd never been
there before and admired the mahogany
paneled walls festooned with evergreen garlands for
Christmas. The well-heeled patrons conducted business
in polite tones, and glasses clinked behind the bar.
George Wickham had said to meet him here at 10pm, but
George was always late.

Making his way toward the bar, Henry congratulated
himself on wearing his navy suit. The St. Regis catered to
a classy clientele, and he appeared to fit in.

"What can I get you, sir?" the bartender asked, wiping
down a glass and placing it on a shelf.

"Hmmm... I'm feeling a Dark 'n' Stormy tonight,"
Henry said.

"Goes with the weather, yes, sir." The bartender started making the drink while keeping a curious eye on Henry.

Henry glanced up at the mural behind the bar – a fiery phoenix swooping skyward from the conflagration of antebellum Atlanta with the 21st century skyline rising near its wing.

"That's... very specific."

The bartender looked over his shoulder. "Yeah, the symbol of Atlanta. A phoenix rising from the ashes."

"*Resurgens*," Henry said.

"Sorry?"

"Oh, uh, the Atlanta motto," Henry said, embarrassed to be touting his education. "'Rising again.' Wish we could all have a do-over, huh?"

"You're tellin' me." The bartender set the drink on the bar, still watching Henry. "Sorry to be staring, sir, but I know I've seen you somewhere before – just can't place where."

Henry was used to this. "I have a familiar face."

"Hold on, you're that guy on that hospital show! The doctor the ladies are always falling for. You're really good, man! Hey, does that happen to you in real life? All those women?"

Henry laughed. "You gotta be careful these days," he said. "I recommend getting consent in writing first – which doesn't go over real well."

The bartender laughed. "You're a hoot, man! 'Get it in writing.' Ha!"

The manager walked by, raising an eyebrow at the bartender who promptly reined himself in.

"Would you like to open a tab, sir?"

"Sure," Henry said, getting out his card.

"Henry, glad you didn't wait for me." George approached the bar, late as ever, and handed the bartender his AmEx. "I'll have what he's having. Put him on my tab."

"George, you don't have to do that."

"You're my guest tonight," George said, surveying the room. "Looks like slim pickings this evening."

"How was Thanksgiving? Did you and Lydia go to the Darcys'?" Henry asked.

"Yep. Thanksgiving and Christmas: the only times I'm allowed to enter the hallowed halls of Pemberley."

"It's so affected to name your house."

"Yes." George took his drink and continued, "Twice a year, I play the contrite brother-in-law, bringing the offering of my good behavior to Fitzwilliam Darcy's altar. I sit there with a smile plastered on my face and watch their family laugh and talk, imagining all the things that could go wrong for them, but never do." He took a drink to chase the bitterness.

"Is that why we're here tonight? You need to blow off some steam?"

"Why else would we be here on a Monday night? Only the most desperate women will be here tonight."

"What women come here to be picked up?"

"Women looking for rich men."

"Well, they're out of luck with you."

"But since I have a room here, they won't know that until tomorrow morning." George took his drink and said, "Let's sit in this corner – we'll have a view of the room."

Henry winced at him. His sister Mary came to mind, and he hoped she was never the target of guys like this. "Things are that bad with Lydia?" he asked, following George to the table.

George grimaced and said, "Same as they've been since Darcy paid me to marry her. Every moment we spend apart is bliss. She was supposed to be entertainment for one weekend ten years ago, and now I'm stuck with her for life."

"Why don't you just divorce her and move on?"

"Are you kidding? Darcy pays my bills! He's paying for our drinks and my room here tonight. There's no way I'm giving that up."

"He pays for you to cheat on his sister-in-law?"

"Henry, he doesn't personally pay my bills. His secretaries do it. And I have an understanding with one of them." George winked and took a sip of his drink. "Do you ever see Maria Bertram?"

Maria Bertram: the mother of Henry's child – whom he never was allowed to see – and the mascot for failure in his life. George had deployed her name and knocked Henry off his high horse as intended. Henry would never recover from his worst mistake. Not only had he seduced and impregnated a married woman, but he had alienated his sister and himself from the entire Bertram family, the best friends they'd ever had.

"George, I never knew you had an interest in ancient history," Henry said, remaining impassive.

"Oh, Henry, please. There should be a hall of fame for that debacle. Your recklessness is a caution to all. I never go for married women."

"That you know of."

"Too complicated. And I don't have any by-blows running around."

"That you know of."

"I'm sure they'd let me know." George took another drink. "I saw Maria Bertram the other day."

"Did you really."

"She looked good."

"I'm sure she did. Like Lydia Bennet, Maria had family she could fall back on. Tom Bertram has paid for —" Henry paused. "— for our son's education and got them a condo near the rest of the family. I think she goes to Ed's church."

"Oh, that's right," George said, pressing his eyes. "Their brother Ed's a preacher. Henry, only you could have managed such a disaster."

"Thank you."

"Here we go," George said, suddenly distracted. "That's what I'm talking about." He leaned forward, a jackal targeting its dinner.

Two women had entered and stood surveying the room with the serenity of the beautiful. They seemed so familiar with this watering hole that Henry got the impression they were the hunters, not the prey. The Christmas spirit had inspired them to coordinate: one wore emerald green with her blonde mane tossed down her back, and the other had selected red heels with her red dress and red lipstick to complement her waves of dramatic, dark hair. Their gazes alighted on George and Henry, watching them appreciatively, and continued around the room in which most conversation had paused as the businessmen noticed them. They moved with practiced grace in their stiletto heels, their silk dresses caressing their hips and fluttering over their cleavage. They chose a place at the bar with room for their admirers to approach and ordered drinks. A honeytrap, Henry thought and smiled.

A man from a nearby group of middle-aged business travelers stood to be the first victim, and they favored him with smiles and exchanged a few pleasantries.

"You know who that is, don't you?" George asked.

"Which one?" Henry said.

"The one in red. That's Isabella Thorpe – Miss Georgia from ten or fifteen years back." He looked at Henry. "Wait – she was in your class at Westerly, wasn't she?"

"Two years younger. My sister's class."

"You know this woman?"

"We're acquainted," Henry said.

"She didn't seem to recognize you."

"She's not here to waste her time on me."

"Oh, you've dated her?"

"No – she's too smart for that. She's only in the market for marriage."

"Yeah, I've heard the whole story," George said, shaking the ice in his drink. "I'm sure you know it better than I do."

"Probably not," Henry said, unwilling to repeat it.

George dove right in. "Wasn't she engaged to some older guy right out of high school? Some friend of her brother's? And right after she won Miss Georgia, she got it in her head she was too good for him. A woman like that could have anybody, and she knew it. She ended up sleeping with one of the Tilney brothers she met at some fundraiser. And he completely ghosted her. Her fiancé found out and ended it. She found somebody else who'd marry her and has been upgrading ever since. Started small, then had an affair with somebody richer and married him."

"Wow, you're quite the expert on this woman you've never met," Henry said. "I'm pretty sure that's not how it happened, George."

"No, it's true. I heard the whole thing from my wife."

"And Lydia is friends with Izzie and has heard her side of the story? I don't think that's how Izzie would describe it."

"What are you, her dad? I'm just saying what happened. Then she had another affair with another guy and married him. That third husband just died and left her millions." George ruminated on all that money as he finished his drink. "After all that hard work, maybe she's finally in the mood for romance."

"She will not be interested in you, George, I'll tell you that right now," Henry said, thinking of his sister Mary again and bristling in women's defense.

Unwilling to ignore this challenge to his manhood, George said, "What do you want to bet? I'll make the stakes low for you. Two hundred dollars says she'll come upstairs with me."

"Let's make it three hundred. She'll turn you down flat."

"What's it to you?"

"You're notorious, George. She knows better than to get mixed up with you. Or me," Henry said.

George smiled. "You're going to lose – and Darcy will thank you for covering the drinks tonight." He lifted a finger for the waiter, and they placed another order.

Another two pigeons had gathered around Isabella and her companion, and Henry turned his attention to the nearby table where the remaining marks laughed and talked.

"Oh, you have got to be kidding me," Henry said under his breath, staring at one of the men who looked up and locked eyes with him. Henry looked away first.

"Is that Tom Bertram?" George asked. "He looks... functional. I thought he was in rehab."

Henry didn't know where to look. "He's been back for months," he said.

"Looks stable now. Though he's in a bar, which seems... inadvisable. How's he doing?"

"What? How should I know?" Henry said, acutely uncomfortable.

"Surely you're in touch, given your... family connection," George said, smirking.

"Turns out you're wrong."

"Really. When was the last time you spoke to Tom?"

"I don't know, ten years ago, maybe?"

"Oh! Then this is awkward for you."

"A little."

"He keeps looking at you."

"Yep, thanks."

Isabella Thorpe's voice wafted their way. George caught the scent and said, "When is she going to get rid of these guys?"

Henry watched Isabella's alluring smile and remembered that look from a theater production they'd done in high school. At that time, the script had called for a kiss – something his high school self never could have achieved offstage. As he watched Isabella play the coquette again, he had the sense this was the last act in a play that had started all those years ago with her pretending love – and would end with... something else. Was this a tragedy or a comedy?

"George Wickham, how are you? It's been a while," someone said, and Henry looked up to find Tom Bertram standing over him, extending his hand to George.

George rose to shake it, and Henry followed suit, struck speechless by the encounter. Would Tom expect him to say something about Maria and his son? Should Henry acknowledge that they hadn't spoken in ten years?

Tom and George exchanged pleasantries, and then Tom turned to Henry.

"Henry."

"Tom."

There was an awkward pause while George looked back and forth between them.

Tom said, "It was orange juice – what I was drinking."

"OK," Henry said. Another pause.

"At Christmas... maybe we'll see you," Tom said.

"Oh – uh. OK."

"I'll be in touch." Tom turned to George. "Great to see you. Y'all have a good night."

George and Henry remained standing, looking at each other as Tom walked out with one of his guests.

"What just happened?" George asked.

Henry couldn't form a coherent thought but felt as if the air were easier to breathe than he remembered.

"You haven't talked to Tom in ten years, and the first thing he says to you is, *It was orange juice?* Why does he care if the guy who knocked up his sister knows whether he's on the wagon or not?" George said.

Henry hazarded a guess. "He just started seeing my sister this week. He's letting me back in, maybe?"

"Tom is dating Mary?" George said. "Plot twist! That is so... Shakespearean. Will *he* impregnate *your* sister, do you think? Like a revenge plot?"

"I don't think so..." Henry said, his mind churning. He looked up to see the blonde in the emerald green dress walking out with one of the men from Tom's table. The remaining admirers stood around Isabella Thorpe so closely that Henry could only see a flash of her red dress or the shine of her dark hair.

George turned to look at the bar and said, disgusted, "Tom distracted me, and now I have to wait for them, too." He resumed his seat and motioned for the waiter. "Oh, well. It'll be entertaining to watch a master at work. I wonder how she'll get rid of them."

The men around Isabella laughed in a wolfish tone familiar to Henry, and he caught sight of her face, wary of her company. His new ease of breathing gave his thoughts focus as he watched her wrap her gauzy stole around her shoulders, obscuring her bosom from their elevated view.

One of them said, "It's too early to close up shop, darlin'," and tore the wrap away, exposing her again. The men hooted and whistled, and one grabbed her wrist as she tried to snatch the shawl back.

Henry stepped toward the group, but George held his arm. "Hold on, Henry. Let's see how she handles it. I'll swoop in and save her in a minute when she's really desperate. Her gratitude will be overwhelming."

Henry pulled his arm away and said, "Bet's off."

"If you sabotage this, you owe me three hundred bucks."

"I'll Venmo you," Henry said.

He approached the men and slapped one on the shoulder with camaraderie. "Hey guys, thanks for keeping her company, but it's time for us to go. Sorry I took so long, Izzie. You ready?"

"Yes, Henry, thank you," Isabella said with dignity.

"I'll take that, sir," Henry said with a charming smile, holding his hand out for the stole. The man who held it seemed uncertain whether he'd been cheated or caught. His leer melted into a pout as he handed the wrap to Henry, who lay it around Isabella's shoulders and gave her his arm.

"Good night!" Henry said to the group and escorted Isabella out of the bar through the marble and gilt foyer to the *porte-cochere*.

Henry stood in the cold with the most beautiful woman he'd ever known still on his arm, uncertain what to do next. The vision of his sister being subjected to that treatment had spurred him to action, and that same sense of protection now prevented him from capitalizing on his advantage. Besides which, the strange conversation with Tom had sparked an idea, suggesting a way back from the solitary life he led.

"Thank you, Henry. That was a masterful performance. Your Emmy is well deserved." Isabella paused before saying, "What now?"

"Hmmm," said Henry, still uncertain how to proceed. He turned to look at her, nearly his height in her three-inch heels, and lost track of time, gazing at her. She wore a scent that invited him closer. As he leaned in, he became aware of the bellmen and made a decision. "What's your address?" he asked, getting out his phone.

"I don't take men home with me."

"Oh, you prefer the St. Regis?" He opened the Uber app. "I'll just see you to your door. It's late."

She looked at him like she'd heard it all before – and then she made a decision. "2880 Rivermeade Drive."

Henry typed it in. "Rivermeade? Those are nice houses over there."

The driver would arrive in two minutes. He felt her shiver next to him and put his suit jacket around her shoulders. He remembered that her elderly husband had died recently and said, "I'm sorry for your loss. I heard your husband passed away."

She pinned him with a skeptical glance, presumably to deflate his mockery, but he looked at her with sympathy.

"Thank you," she said before searching through her handbag for a place to hide her emotion.

He couldn't drag his eyes away. Her beauty had deepened and ripened since high school. His eyes caressed the line of her face as she looked back up at him.

"Why are you staring, Henry? You've seen me before."

"You're bringing to mind a poem I haven't thought of in a long time," he said. "Did you read this in Mr. Morgan's English class? When he read it to us, I thought someone had written it about you – until I saw it was Byron.

> *She walks in beauty, like the night*
> *Of cloudless climes and starry skies,*
> *And all that is best of dark and bright*
> *Meet in her aspect and her eyes,*

59

Thus mellowed to that tender light
Which heaven to gaudy day denies."

"It's been a long time since someone quoted me poetry, Henry." Isabella blushed but held his gaze. "You're very good at this," she added to remind him of her immunity to charm.

Or to remind herself? Henry wondered.

But Henry wasn't in the mood for banter. Something too important was happening, and he didn't want to lose it. In a moment, he had risen from the ashes of a night out with George Wickham, sparked to life by Tom's hinted invitation to Christmas, and now found himself rejuvenated in Isabella's presence.

The car pulled up, and he opened the door, taking his jacket and assisting her into the back seat. She slid over to make room for him, but he leaned in and said to her, "Don't come here anymore, Izzie. You're too good for this. Go home," and closed the door, waving the driver on.

Resurgens.

Vignette 7

GREAT NEWS

*In which Aunt Norris receives great news
at the oncologist*

"Maria always remembers to bring my medications. You're supposed to bring them to every appointment."

A volley of wet coughs prevented Mrs. Norris from spouting further criticism. She slouched in her wheelchair, her claw gripping the handle of her portable oxygen machine, and scowled in her misery.

Fanny Bertram sat with her aunt in the oncologist's examination room and looked at her sour, wrinkled face. Not dignifying the complaint with a reply, Fanny thought about something she'd heard somewhere – was it George Orwell or Coco Chanel? *At fifty, you have the face you deserve.* Her Aunt Norris' wrinkled face at the age of sixty-five was a map of bitterness. An unhappy marriage from dominating her husband had left trenches between her eyes. Her lips, so often tightened in disapproval, now sagged at the corners toward her chin like the oxbow of a river.

Mrs. Norris drew a crackling breath, coughed again, and then wheezed, "Maria should have been here. I don't like it when you come – you flirt with the doctor."

Fanny had long accustomed herself to Aunt Norris' gibes and remained calm. Her husband Edmund, her cousins Tom, Maria, and Julia, both her Aunt and Uncle Bertram – everyone bristled in Fanny's defense when Aunt Norris started needling her. But Fanny had decided that her worth did not hinge on Aunt Norris' approval and never bothered to defend herself.

Mrs. Norris tried a different tack. Fanny would sometimes rise to someone else's defense, so she said, "I don't like Dr. Willoughby's nurse. She's fat and impolite."

"But not deaf. Her work station is right next door."

"I don't care if she hears me or not."

"You'll care when she gives you your radiation shot later."

"It always hurts more when she gives the shot because she doesn't warm it up enough. I want you to ask for the other nurse to do it."

"Or we could ask this lady to warm it up for you earlier."

"You're not the one who has to have the shot. Maria does what I tell her to do. Why didn't Maria bring me?"

And we're back, Fanny thought. Aunt Norris knew that Maria had a terrible cold and couldn't come. This twenty-year-long comparison Mrs. Norris liked to maintain between Fanny and Maria Bertram no longer hurt like it did when Fanny was ten years old, a lesser cousin living in the Bertrams' stately Atlanta home. Those wounds had long healed and wouldn't reopen no matter how much Aunt Norris liked to pick them.

The *knock, knock* finally came, and the door opened on the barely overweight nurse in a KN95 mask who said, "How are you today, Mrs. Norris?" as if she already knew the answer. She took Aunt Norris' vitals while saying, "Uh-huh" every once in a while in response to the stream of vitriol.

"I'm dying! That's how I'm doing today!" Aunt Norris coughed without covering her mouth, which made Fanny's skin crawl, and continued in her cracked voice. "The steroids keep me awake at night, and that other drug gives me constant diarrhea. And I can't walk more than a few steps before getting dizzy. You people aren't doing your job! I've never been a smoker. There is no reason I should have lung cancer. Why can't you figure it out?"

The nurse put the thermometer under Aunt Norris' tongue, and the room became abruptly quiet. The oxygen machine pumped and hissed.

"Your temperature is a bit elevated today, Mrs. Norris. Are you having any unusual symptoms?"

"More unusual than not being able to breathe?" She coughed productively. "Yes, there's all this green mucus." She showed a heavy tissue to the nurse.

"Mmmm-hmmmm. That's pretty nasty, Mrs. Norris. Dr. Willoughby will be right in. You be sure to show that to him," the nurse said with a suppressed smile.

"Chastity, would you mind warming up my aunt's medicine for the shot later? It hurts more when it's straight out of the fridge," Fanny said.

"Yes ma'am, I'll be sure to do that." Chastity closed the door behind her.

"I wanted the other nurse to give me the shot. I told you that."

"I thought that would be rude to ask." Fanny reached in her tote bag and pulled out her laptop. "I hope you don't mind if I work on my children's book, Aunt Norris. My deadline is in a few days, and I have to finish these revisions."

There was silence for a while apart from the oxygen machine as Fanny worked and Mrs. Norris stared in front of her, her mouth twitching in thought. "I don't know why little Eddie likes your books so much. There's nothing to them," she said.

"Oh, you've read them?"

Mrs. Norris shifted in her seat. "He asks me to read them to him sometimes when I babysit for Maria."

"I'm so happy he likes them! Thank you for reading to him. That reminds me of that poem by Strickland Gillilan:

> *You may have tangible wealth untold;*
> *Caskets of jewels and coffers of gold.*

Richer than I you can never be –
I had a Mother who read to me."

"Ha! I would bet you anything my sister never read to you." Mrs. Norris payed for her mirth with a fit of coughing.

"No, you're right. She never had time. And Maria never has time to read to Eddie either. But you read to all of us when we were young – and now you read to Eddie. It's an invaluable gift. Your life and your time are a gift."

That was hard for Fanny to say since she'd been excluded from story hour and had hearkened from across the room – but those books Aunt Norris had read to the Bertram children had fired her imagination and made her the writer she had become.

Mrs. Norris had no response to that and glowered while Fanny went back to work. The *knock, knock* came again, and the doctor appeared.

John Willoughby's charisma filled the room as he favored the ladies with a gorgeous smile. His teasing gaze rested on Fanny, and he said, "Mrs. Bertram, you look as beautiful as ever today. How are you?"

Fanny rolled her eyes and shook her head to dismiss the compliment. "I'm great, thanks, Dr. Willoughby – how is your family? Did y'all have fun at Disney World?"

"Oh, yeah, Jeez – the kids loved it. We all had a great time. Have you been there since they've added –"

"Hello?" Mrs. Norris said. "We're here for my appointment? I'm drowning in green mucus, and you're flirting with my niece? She's a pastor's wife! You have no shame!"

Dr. Willoughby gazed at Fanny. "Mrs. Bertram, how did I not know this about you? I may have to start coming to church!"

"My husband would love to meet you, Dr. Willoughby." Fanny smirked at him and opened a new document on her laptop to take notes for the appointment. Mrs. Norris held the tissue with the green sputum toward the doctor.

"That – wow. That is disgusting, Mrs. Norris." He picked up the trash can and offered it to her.

"You don't want to examine it or test it or something?" Mrs. Norris said, disappointed to throw away such a fine specimen.

"We would need a fresh sample – and it seems there is plenty more where that came from," he said as she began coughing into a new tissue.

He logged into his computer portal and scrolled through Mrs. Norris' bloodwork results. "Alright, the bloodwork looks normal. I mean, not normal – you have cancer – but it's no worse than usual. Well, it's a little worse than usual. Where is that report for your 6-month CT scan...? You had the scan yesterday, right?" He kept clicking and scrolling. "Awww, the radiologist hasn't interpreted it yet. Arrrgh! Alright. Lemme take a look here...."

After double-clicking and comparing the image to a previous one, Dr. Willoughby's breezy manner became still. He felt for his phone, searched for a number, and placed a call.

Fanny expected some commentary from Aunt Norris – but Mrs. Norris had become quiet, as well, and seemed uncharacteristically placid.

"Yeah, hi Pam. Have you seen Jane Norris' CT scan from yesterday? No – no report yet, but you won't need one. Can you pull it up and take a look?" He turned to Mrs. Norris. "This is your pulmonologist. I just want a second set of eyes on this real quick."

Mrs. Norris continued to sit quietly. Fanny was distracted from the suspenseful consultation by Aunt Norris' lack of reaction. It felt as if her aunt had suddenly gone deaf or become senile – as if her aunt had been replaced. Fanny risked a light touch on her shoulder to see if she were still there – and Aunt Norris nodded in acknowledgement.

"That's what I see, too – just wanted to check. Yes, she's in the room with me right now. I'll tell her." There was a pause. "I'm an oncologist, Pam. I got this."

Dr. Willoughby put his phone back in his pocket and swiveled his stool to face the ladies. "Mrs. Norris," he said, clasping his hands between his knees. "Funny story from med school: I was doing my oncology rotation, and the doctor in charge asked us if we knew on average what percentage of his patients die. Now he was the leading oncologist at MD Anderson in Houston, so we knew he was the best and had saved a ton of patients, so the death rate must be lower than other doctors'. *20%*, someone said. *80%*, someone else said – pretty disrespectfully, I thought. That seemed high to me. 50%, I said. What's your guess, Mrs. Norris? What percentage of the leading oncologist's patients die?"

Mrs. Norris breathed in and out, looking at Dr. Willoughby – in and out again.

"100%," she said.

"That's right! 100% of his patients die. Because... because we're all going to die... and no matter how smart the doctor, there's nothing we can do to stop that." He took a deep breath and leaned toward her. "You were told two years ago that you had cancer. We've tried multiple drugs and several therapies. We had hope that the radiation treatments would stop the growth, but they haven't. And now... this is the point where I tell you... that I have nothing else to offer... except my sincere apologies that there's nothing more I can do."

There was silence for several seconds before Mrs. Norris said, "Well, you can tell Pam that you did very well. I assume you give that speech often?"

"Almost daily. 100% of my patients die, too, in spite of my handsome face. But you're my first patient to guess 100%! There should be a prize or something."

"My aunt has held the hands of many dying people over the years. She was a pastor's wife, too – a long time ago," Fanny said.

Dr. Willoughby's eyebrows rose as he searched for something to say. "That... surprises me. I would not have guessed that."

"Why? Because I'm not like Miss Goodie-Two-Shoes here?" Mrs. Norris hacked and coughed.

"Uhhhh...you are now out of my area of expertise. I think the next step is for me to send in our patient care liaison to discuss hospice options." He stood and faced Mrs. Norris. "Let's make an appointment for six weeks from now, and I hope to see you then, Mrs. Norris. Y'all enjoy your Christmas. Mrs. Bertram, always a pleasure." He winked at Fanny and left.

The two women sat in silence for several moments.

"I'm sorry, Aunt Norris," Fanny said.

"What are you sorry for?" Mrs. Norris said in her usual, combative tone.

"For this news." Fanny paused and then said, "This will be a significant Christmas for all of us."

"If I make it til then."

"Of course, you will! We have to celebrate Christmas with you and remember together... to remember... why we mourn differently than other people."

Mrs. Norris appeared to swallow something bitter. "What's that thing you're always saying?"

"What thing?"

"How it's good that... it doesn't matter how imperfect we are –"

"Oh. In the end, it doesn't matter how good we are – it only matters how good Jesus is."

"Well... this is the end."

"Hmmmm." Fanny waited for further revelation and then said, "What do you think about that?"

"I think I haven't been good enough." Mrs. Norris covered her emotion with a volley of coughs.

"Me either."

Mrs. Norris looked at her incredulously and saw that Fanny was perfectly serious.

"Well if you're not good enough, who is?"

"You know who is."

Mrs. Norris wheezed and crackled and heaved angry breaths. She coughed into another tissue and pitched it toward the trash can where it stuck just shy of the rim. She and Fanny watched it hang and stretch for the ground and finally drop to the floor. Fanny started chuckling, and Mrs. Norris cracked a laugh – and then they both started giggling until Mrs. Norris couldn't breathe anymore and coughs overcame her again. Fanny took a clean tissue and collected the specimen from the floor, dropped it in the bin and thoroughly sanitized her hands, smiling at her Aunt Norris.

"I'm sorry, Fanny," Mrs. Norris said in a croaking voice.

"It's fine – that was hilarious."

"No." She coughed. "I'm sorry – for thinking you weren't good enough."

"Oh, I'm not. I have to rely on Jesus completely."

"No, no, no," she wheezed. "I mean for thinking you weren't good enough for our family. For the way –" She coughed and choked and forced herself to say, "– I treated you."

Tears pricked Fanny's eyes. That apology was the final healing balm on the old wound – and Fanny loved her for it. She knelt down next to the wheelchair and hugged her aunt for the first time in her life.

Mrs. Norris stiffened under the assault and then patted her on the back in an unpracticed way. "Alright. Alright. That's – that's nice. Maybe I should have said that sooner."

Fanny returned to her chair and wiped her eyes.

Mrs. Norris stared ahead of her. "Christmas is in 3 weeks – that should be enough time."

"For what?"

"There are people I should... say things to." She concentrated on her breathing for a few minutes, absorbing the oxygen from the cannula that dried out her nose. "Christmas," she said and adjusted the tubing that pressed into her cheeks. "Fanny, sing 'O Little Town of Bethlehem' for me."

"What, right now?"

"No, after I'm dead. Sing it now!"

"I only know the first verse."

"What kind of a pastor's wife are you?" She sniffed in frustration. "Look it up on your phone!" *You idiot* was implied.

Fanny found the lyrics and began to sing softly with Mrs. Norris attempting to harmonize in her cracked voice. When the patient care liaison paused outside the door to knock, she heard the quavering voices and the words,

> *O Holy child of Bethlehem,*
> *Descend to us, we pray;*
> *Cast out our sin and enter in;*
> *Be born in us today!*

We hear the Christmas angels
The great glad tidings tell;
O come to us, abide with us,
Our Lord Emmanuel!

Vignette 8

PERSUASION

In which Anne Wentworth won't allow it

E linor Dashwood-Ferrars accepted a claim ticket
from the valet and walked ahead of her mother
and two sisters into Canterbury Court, one of
Atlanta's luxury senior living communities. The
Christmas lights over the door winked in a failed attempt
to raise her Christmas spirit. The four Dashwood ladies
had convened to preview this place for Mrs. Dashwood at
what was supposed to be a stress-free Christmas service
held for the residents – but thanks to Marianne, as
usual, they were late. Adding hassle to hustle, Elinor's
husband Ward (an Episcopalian minister on the board
of this institution) was leading the service that would
begin in five minutes – and had forgotten his notes, now
in Elinor's possession. At the front desk, she signed their
names and accepted four visitor badges while her sisters

continued an argument begun in the car with their mother.

Marianne was saying, "...but his *sisters* will be there! Meg is not going to 'spend the night with a man!' She's been invited – by his parents – to their annual Christmas gathering and will be sharing a room with his *sisters*! What is there to object to?"

Elinor gave Marianne the look that said *lower your voice* and mechanically put a lanyard over each of their heads as if they were children.

Mrs. Dashwood brushed Elinor's hand away before her coiffure was disturbed and arranged her own visitor tag over her cashmere sweater set. "We are not well-acquainted with their family. Meg has met this boy twice –"

"Three times, Mom. We met at church and have been out twice since," Meg said.

"– which is not long enough to know someone before taking the momentous step of meeting his family and spending the night –" she floundered, "– in his presence!"

"Mom!" Marianne and Meg groaned in unison as Elinor gathered them like sheep and herded them down the hallway, past the large reception room decorated for Christmas like the drawing room of someone's ancestral home, past the dining room that overlooked the extensive gardens, down a second hallway to the second set of elevators on the way to the garden-level chapel.

Elinor attempted to remind them why they were there with comments like, "This dining room is pleasant

74

– lots of light during the day from these windows." And "Look at those gorgeous gardens, Mom. The residents get their own plots – you wouldn't have to give up gardening." And, "It's not too long a walk for someone like you – you're still in such good shape." She ran out of things to say at the elevator and punched the call button.

Meg brought the conversation back to her proposed weekend away. "His parents rent a bunch of cabins at Callaway Gardens, and all ten siblings and their spouses and children come every year for this Christmas gathering! Everyone brings whomever they're dating to introduce them to the family –"

"That is exactly my point," interrupted Mrs. Dashwood, returning to the discussion with vigor. "It is too soon for him to introduce you to his family as if... as if..."

"As if your baby were grown up, Mom?" Marianne said.

Mrs. Dashwood was prevented from responding by the arrival of a family friend and her elderly father at the elevator door.

"Hi, y'all!" the woman said.

"Anne, hi!" Elinor said, relieved by the interruption. "And Mr. Elliot – I wondered if we would see you at the chapel service tonight. Mom is thinking about moving here, so we brought her to the Christmas hymn-sing." She gave the illuminated button another jab and said, "Ward is downstairs already and needs these notes. Have you settled into your new apartment yet, Mr. Elliot?"

Mr. Elliot dismissed the question with an airy wave of his liver-spotted hand. "I certainly don't intend to *settle* here. This is a brief stay while my health recovers. I'll be moving back to my home in Tuxedo Park soon."

"Oh!" Mrs. Dashwood looked at Anne. "I didn't think they had short-term stays here – you buy into this community, don't you?"

Anne was nodding her head with a long-suffering expression that said, *There's no point in correcting him.* She tapped the illuminated call button. "This elevator is so slow, you're not even aware it's moving. That's if you ever get on it."

The doors began to slide apart with majestic torpidity, as if they guarded the hereafter no longer bound by time. When a large enough space cleared, a wizened little man in exercise clothes shuffled out while Elinor checked her phone. The group parted to let him through, exchanging Merry Christmases with him, as Elinor held the elevator door for everyone – not that any danger existed of it closing precipitately. Inside, she pressed Garden level and mashed the closed door button.

The reverse procedure began as Elinor took a deep breath and wondered if this elevator existed for her personal sanctification. Mr. Elliot and Mrs. Dashwood chatted while the others discussed Meg's new boyfriend.

"We met at church over Thanksgiving weekend!" Meg said. "He's a senior at Georgia Tech and is going to be an astrophysicist! He's waiting to hear back from several PhD programs. He has *nine siblings* and has invited me to his family's Christmas retreat next weekend! Anne, it's such a pleasure to be pursued by a man who knows what he wants and has purpose and drive. He's not one of those guys whose parents arrange everything for him. He has multiple jobs to pay for college and is *doing* something with his life!"

The elevator had almost closed when a man's voice from the hallway said, "Hold the door, please!"

Anne inserted her hand between the panels, and they slowly began to open again, eliciting an involuntary cry from Elinor. The widening space revealed a hint of an enormous flower arrangement, and the delivery man said "thank you" from behind the red and green extravaganza.

"Being a self-made man is one thing," Mrs. Dashwood said, joining Meg and Anne's conversation as they waited for the doors to open, "but I don't know that I want you to be connected to a family that has so little..."

"Here we go!" Marianne said to Anne.

"So little to recommend them!" Mrs. Dashwood insisted.

"This is what I told you," Marianne said. "The family isn't good enough for Mom. They need to be rich enough to pay for the higher education of all ten children. And, frankly, having ten children is tacky. Also," she began to whisper, "I think they have ancestors who weren't from our zip code."

The flower arrangement squeezed into a corner of the elevator where the man behind it said, "Thank you! Sorry to hold y'all up. This elevator takes forever, and I would have been out there all night."

"No problem," Anne said. "That's a gorgeous arrangement! Where are you going with it?"

"It's for the lobby downstairs. They're putting one of these in every lobby this week."

"Where's it from? It's really beautiful."

"Firwoods on East Andrews."

"That's the store that his brother owns!" Meg exclaimed in delight.

The flower arrangement whipped aside, narrowly missing Mr. Elliot's eye, and revealed a young man's astonished face topped by a mass of black curls. He'd heard the joy in Meg's voice and smiled like he'd won a national election. The air electrified as the two young people stood two-and-a-half feet apart, fighting the magnetism generated by the presence of the beloved. Everyone in the elevator car fell silent watching this eloquent display of adoration.

Mrs. Dashwood looked back and forth between them and said, "Aren't you going to introduce me, Meg?"

Recovering first, the man said, "Mrs. Dashwood, forgive me. I'm Zachary Morland. I believe my sister Catherine Tilney is a friend of your elder daughters – Elinor and Marianne, right?" he asked, smiling at the women. "I'm glad for this chance to meet you and ask personally if you would allow Meg to join my family for our annual Christmas retreat next weekend. We have a whole cabin for the girls, so she'll be well taken care of."

Mrs. Dashwood blinked several times, bowled over by his confidence, and murmured that she would have to think about that.

"Of course! I'll keep a spot in my sisters' cabin reserved for her, and I'll check back with you later this week."

The doors began to open on the garden level floor, which surprised everyone since no one had felt the car move. To cover the possible awkwardness of watching the children stare at each other again while trapped by the glacial parting of the doors, Anne said, "I know Catherine, too! We haven't run into each other in a while, but I follow her on Instagram. Please say hello to her for me. I'm Anne Wentworth, and this is my father Walter Elliot."

The doors clunked into place, and Elinor said, "It's nice to meet you, Zach," before speeding down the hall to the chapel where her husband had just begun the opening prayer. Marianne hooked her mother's arm, determined to rush her away from Meg and Zach – but Mrs. Dashwood would not dash.

She stepped out of the elevator and said, "Meg, we're late for the Christmas chapel. Come with me, please."

Meg appeared unable to overcome the gravitational pull of Zach's presence. They walked out of the elevator together, and he said to her with a gentle smile, "I'll see you soon." To Mrs. Dashwood, he said, "I look forward to seeing you again, ma'am. You have a beautiful family," as he smiled at Marianne. And to Anne Wentworth – "Anne, I'll let Catherine know you said hello. It was nice to meet you, Mr. Elliot." And with a parting smile for Meg, he carried the towering arrangement to the garden lobby.

The group stood in silence for a moment until he was out of earshot – then Meg said, "Isn't he wonderful, Mom? I want you to like him! You will see how incredible he is!"

Mrs. Dashwood sputtered in confusion and appealed to Anne for help. "You understand, Anne. You come from the same background – how would your father have felt if you had..." Mrs. Dashwood trailed off as she remembered that Anne *had* married a man against her father's wishes – someone from the *nouveau riche* whose money (and family's manners) came from trucking, she recalled – or was it shipping? Mrs. Dashwood glanced at Mr. Elliot, but he seemed sublimely unaware of the conversation, waiting patiently for the ladies to proceed. The melody of "O Come, O Come Emmanuel" wafted down the hall.

"Mrs. Dashwood..." Anne said, pausing. "In my experience – which I'm sure you recall – my family persuaded me to reject Frederick because of his family background – and I mourned my choice for eight years. Until – by an act of God – I was given a second chance to say yes!" Anne took a breath, considering her words. "Unlike me, Meg knows her own mind and is not a persuadable person," she said, eyeing Meg's set jaw and determined expression. She smiled with sympathy at Mrs. Dashwood. "You love your daughters so much and have reared them to make good decisions. If that young man she met at church is the one she's set her heart on – I'd say you've done a great job!"

Mrs. Dashwood adjusted her pearls and twisted her rings as the compliments worked on her.

Anne saw the signs of weakening and added, "The best thing about this weekend away with his family is that she will either fit right in or never want to see him again. If you're convinced he's not right for her, then letting her go could work in your favor."

At that, Mrs. Dashwood stopped fussing with her jewelry and looked at Meg, whose face radiated hope. She reached toward her daughter and tucked an errant curl behind Meg's ear.

"Mom?" Meg said.

Mrs. Dashwood sighed and said, "Alright. You can go."

"Thank you, thank you, thank you, Mom!!" Meg said in a muted scream that accounted for the Christmas service down the hall. She threw her arms around her mother's neck. "I have to go tell him. He must still be here."

"You are coming with me into this service now. You can tell him later."

"Oh, Mom!"

"*Now*, Meg. Don't push me."

"Alright," Meg said and pulled herself together.

Marianne looked at Anne with awe at what her friend had accomplished and steered her mother toward the chapel.

As Mrs. Dashwood walked away, Meg hugged Anne and said, "You have made me the happiest girl in the world, and I'm naming my first child after you."

Anne laughed and took her father's arm, leading him toward the music. As they snuck into the chapel festooned with garlands and wreaths and twinkling with lights, Mr. Elliot demonstrated some level of attention to the conversation, if not awareness of his surroundings, when he said loudly, "I named my first child Elizabeth after the Queen of England."

Elinor glared at Anne and Meg as they giggled all the way to their seats.

Vignette 9

PARADOX

*In which Henry Crawford's worst mistake
becomes his greatest joy*

"Ring the doorbell."

"You're closer. You ring it."

Mary and Henry Crawford stood on the limestone terrace outside Mr. and Mrs. Bertram's Italianate mansion in Atlanta, facing the front door on Christmas Eve. A large wreath bristled with pine cones and live poinsettias, which made Henry wonder if they paid for a fresh wreath every day.

"Are you gonna ring it?" Henry said to his sister. "This is ridiculous. We've been here hundreds of times. We practically grew up here."

"We left ten years ago, Henry. A lot has happened since then," Mary said pointedly. "You're not ringing it either."

"Well, we can't just stand here."

"Apparently, we can."

For the thousandth time, Henry confronted the disaster that had estranged them from the Bertrams a decade previously – from these kind people who had unofficially adopted them after their parents' sudden death. Unable to move past this story or to rewrite the ending, he dwelled on the Bertrams' recriminations, justly deserved after he'd seduced their eldest daughter Maria – and gotten her pregnant. He shook his head, thinking of Maria's subsequent divorce and the ruination of the life she had so carefully built – entirely due to his arrogance. That debacle burned in his chest as he clutched a wrapped present he'd brought for his 10-year-old son.

"Ring it, Mary."

"You ring it. I can't."

Mary turned toward the boxwood shrubberies off the terrace and rolled her eyes. Never would she outlive the embarrassment over her attempted seduction of Tom Bertram, the eldest son, when she was in high school. She glanced up at her former bedroom window next to the copper drain pipe and remembered what she'd been wearing the night she'd texted him in his dorm room at Georgia Tech. He had come home and climbed the drain pipe to her window so he wouldn't awaken anyone. The household would have remained ignorant had the pipe not broken – and had he not fallen two stories into the shrubs, barely missing the terrace balustrade. Mary had screamed, rousing the family, who discovered Tom wallowing in the crushed landscaping, unscathed because of his spectacular drunkenness.

Following her own train of thought, she said, "It'll be funny having a dry Christmas Eve. Tom said everyone insisted on mocktails and virgin eggnog to lash him to the wagon. You don't care, right?"

"Right now, that is the last thing I care about," Henry said. "Though, come to think of it, I was counting on a few drinks to get me through this."

"Another thing I forgot to tell you." Mary squeezed the bag of potpourri she had brought in lieu of a bottle of wine, and it crackled in its cellophane as she stalled.

"Yes?"

"Maria is engaged, and her fiancé will be here." To head off any reaction from Henry, she hurried on. "I know that's a relief since there will be no suggestion that y'all should pick back up where you left off or anything."

"You know what?" said Henry. "I can't do this."

"What?"

"Nope. Can't do it. It was great of Tom to invite me – that was a nice gesture since you and he are now... But I should have heard from Maria before coming. She's the one I.... There's no way she wants me here with her fiancé."

"Why? Because you're so handsome?"

Henry turned to face her. "I ruin everything, Mary."

"You're just scared of seeing your son."

"Yeah, well, you know," Henry said, turning the present over in his hands, "I haven't ever seen him except that one time when I ran into Maria at the mall five years ago. And she looked terrified the whole time we were standing there like I was going to tell Eddie who I was – which I didn't." He coughed to cover a heavy sigh and cleared his throat. "This is too awkward, and I can't do it." Henry turned back toward the car just as the front door swung open.

Henry wheeled around as if a gun had fired and confronted the siblings Tom and Maria Bertram in the open doorway.

Maria said, "Y'all. Seriously. You know we have security cameras, right? We've all been in there taking bets on how long you'd stand out here in the cold, but I couldn't take it anymore. Henry, you're not going to ruin anything – it was my idea to invite you. We have audio, too."

Maria looked up at her brother Tom who gazed at Mary with such longing that he missed his cue.

"Uh, Tom?" Maria said. "Are you going to invite them in?"

"Yes – please," Tom said, awakening to his duties and holding out his hand to Mary.

She took it and stepped inside, turning back to Henry. "Henry, come on."

But Henry didn't come. "Y'all, I'm sorry. I... this isn't going to work. Would you give this to Eddie and tell him... tell him I'm sorry."

There was a clatter of footsteps on the marble floor inside, and four or five children weaseled their way between the adults on their way out to the expansive lawn. One of them stopped when he saw Henry and said, "Hey! You're my dad!"

Henry was struck speechless by this encounter with his fourth grade self. The child was tall for his age and remarkably handsome with the same hair, eyes, nose – and captivating smile.

"He's seen you on TV," Maria said.

"Is that for me?" the child asked, pointing to the present Henry still held.

"Yes. Yes, it is," Henry managed to say.

"Eddie, come on!!" the other children called from the lawn.

"I'll put it under the tree for you, Eddie. You run on and play. You'll have plenty of time with your dad later," Maria said, taking the present from Henry.

"See you later!" Eddie said and sprinted toward the others.

"He knows about me?" Henry said.

"Yeah, I told him the whole story just a couple months ago."

"You told a ten-year-old the whole story?"

"Oh, now you're going to start parenting, Henry?" Maria said with a smile.

"Noooo. No, no. No. I just... What did you tell him exactly?"

"You know, I would have grabbed my coat if I'd thought we were going to have this conversation in the cold, so I'm just going to make this fast because I can tell you're not going to come inside 'til we get past this." She chaffed her arms and shivered. "I told him that I was

87

married a long time ago to a man my whole family told me I shouldn't have married. We had nothing in common – except the money that I married him for – and I was very unhappy. The right thing to do would have been to make the best of it and learn to love him – he wasn't bad, just terribly stupid, I told Eddie."

Henry scoffed at the memory of that hapless husband of Maria's whom he had duped – and then remembered to be ashamed and looked down to hide his smile.

Maria continued, shivering. "I then told Eddie that I made another big mistake attempting to correct the first one. I wanted to escape from my marriage, so I targeted a good friend who was very handsome and pretended I was married to him instead. It was wrong, and I shouldn't have done it, but a great thing came from it – I got to have Eddie!"

With his head still bowed, Henry looked up at Maria under his brows and said, "So *you* targeted *me*? That's very generous of you not to make me the villain of the story."

"I only told the truth, Henry. Sorry if it emasculates you, but I invited the whole affair. It was wrong – and I'm sorry."

"*You're* sorry? *I'm* sorry!"

"Yeah, I know. And as a woman, I've definitely borne the brunt of the scandal while your career has been built on your bad-boy reputation. (Congratulations on your Emmy, by the way.) But the fact is – women have the greater responsibility because we have the greater *ability*. We can create life. What's an Emmy compared to *that*, right?" she said, indicating their son on the lawn.

Henry turned to look at Eddie throwing the football to his cousins – shouting "Go long! Go long!" – and frowned in wonder. "So... everything we did was wrong... but it turned out right?" he asked Maria. "We're good?"

"Well... it's funny you put it that way, but..." She shivered again and said, "Look, this is the last thing I'll say before we go inside and have some hot chocolate and hope I don't get sick: Wrong being made right is the meaning of Christmas. It's happened to me, and I invited you tonight because I want you to hear the good news, too: nothing you've done, no matter how horrible, is bigger than Jesus' love for you."

Tom interjected, "She just converted and joined Ed's church earlier this year and can't stop talking about Jesus. Don't let it put you off. Come inside, Henry. I'm freezing."

It had grown darker as they stood there, and without realizing it, Henry had stepped toward the familiar, warm marble hall, decorated for Christmas, twinkling with lights. He joined his adopted family inside and said, "You don't let him watch me in the series that was released this week, do you? It's a little mature, don't you think?"

"I think that you don't get to parent yet, Henry. Let's get through tonight first, ok? Come meet my fiancé!" Maria said, leading the way, as Tom shut the door on the cold.

Vignette 10

SEVEN SWANS
A-SWIMMING

*In which Isabella Thorpe and
Henry Crawford find Christmas*

"Henry! Where's your drink? Get over here!"
Henry Crawford barely caught his name
over the band. In the flashing lights of the
ballroom, he turned to see a group of his old high school
classmates gathered around a table near the dance floor.
This was Henry's first time attending the Apogee Town
Club's annual New Year's Eve Fairy Tale Ball – and he
laughed at how absurd his 36-year-old friends looked in
their Prince Charming costumes. Not a member of this
club, Henry had been invited as a celebrity to emcee the
evening's fundraiser for the Children's Hospital of
Atlanta. He smiled at his friends and raised a hand in

acknowledgement as he finished with a group of women who had gathered around him.

"Have you done many period dramas before? That rake you play in this new one is so cruel!" one woman was shouting above the band. "So different from the doctor in that hospital series. Which character is more like you, do you think?"

Another woman who imagined herself a provocateur interjected, "They both look the same with their shirt off – how different is one character from another, really."

Henry eyed the second woman, dressed as a sexy villain of some sort, while answering the first. "There's a bit of cruelty in all of us, don't you think? It's actually easy and fun to play the bad guy – because you get to act on your worst instincts and get away with it, right?"

"Is that right! I never thought about it that way before!" the first woman said, beaming up at Henry.

"So, Mr. Crawford, it's less fun playing the good guy?" the second woman asked, raising her alluring shoulders, as the other ladies sparkled at him.

Henry knew he embodied Adonis in his tailored tuxedo and accepted that these women had all ogled him shirtless on multiple streaming services on many occasions. What they had never seen and could never appreciate was the most-exercised muscle in his body – the one that kept his eyes elevated to theirs instead of on their cleavage, tauntingly displayed under his view. Anyone who glanced at the exposed flesh received a poor grade: C for Creep. So he looked the provocative woman in the eye and gave her what she wanted: He smiled and winked.

"No fun at all," he said, and she seemed to billow under his (censored) admiration.

"Mr. Crawford?" A member of the staff spoke over the women's heads. "Please excuse me. It's twenty minutes 'til midnight. Just wanted to make sure you have what you need before the countdown."

"Thank you," Henry said. "Please excuse me, ladies. I need to get ready. It was a pleasure talking with you."

They all smiled and waved – the provocateur winked back – and Henry made his way toward the nearest exit from the ballroom. He played the part of emcee well, with friendly smiles and waves for the club members and sympathetic eyebrow lifts for the waiters as he walked at the perfect speed, conveying purpose without panic. Everyone watched him, and no one stopped him – he congratulated himself on his masterful exit and headed down an atmospherically lit hallway looking for an empty room. A throng of women approached and would intercept him before he reached the men's room, just in view – so he backed into a door that said "Staff Only" and hid in the service stairwell until they passed.

Fifteen minutes remained until the countdown, for which his convivial smile and raised glass were required on stage – plenty of time to take a breather if he could avoid friends and fans. He heard the women pass the door on their way to the ladies' room.

One of them said, "Wasn't that Henry Crawford? Where did he go?"

Another replied, "I wonder who he'll end up with tonight. My money's on Isabella Thorpe. She's between husbands again, bless her heart."

Another said, "Sandy, hush!" before the gossip continued in the inner sanctum of the powder room.

Henry rolled his eyes and sighed. Poor Izzy Thorpe – hadn't she been through enough without having her name linked with his? He knew all the facts about his high school friend – how she'd been engaged to a man whom she betrayed before the wedding 15 years before; how she'd then married a series of wealthy men – the last of whom had just died, leaving her millions. The last husband (and maybe the second?) had been a member of the Apogee Club, and Henry had wondered if she'd be there that evening. There was no sign of her yet. He had spoken to her only a few times since high school — the last time, at the St. Regis Hotel bar just a few weeks previously when he'd behaved rather well – and had thought of her every day since.

He could still hear people milling around outside and checked his watch. Ten more minutes. Though lacking in comfortable club chairs, this hiding place would serve as well as any to be alone before the next exertion – so he leaned into the corner, crossing his arms, and faced the stairwell. The Izzy Thorpe he knew in high school – without question, the most beautiful woman he'd ever known (and he'd known some) – could have charmed any man to do anything. But he'd always thought her infamous career had developed out of desperation rather than a love of power or money. She was abandoned in every sense of the word – by her dead father, her alcoholic mother, jealous friends and bitter sisters who couldn't approach her beauty, mothers at her high school who should have welcomed her into their homes instead of turning a chipped shoulder. He'd watched it happen repeatedly in high school – his own sister Mary had been one of her jealous classmates – and knew that Izzy would eventually abandon her self-respect in an urgent pursuit of love and security.

He adjusted his shoulder against the wall and thought how he wanted to give her those things and shield her from gossip – but association with him would only stain her further. His life hadn't yet received the gloss of marriage. He had broken up a marriage, if that counted, and had a son with a childhood friend whose life he had derailed, and had participated in innumerable, forgettable couplings, all splashed across the internet. It would not be kind to cast Izzy as his next fling, though that's not how he thought of her – and no longer how he thought of himself.

The light on the upstairs landing was out, and a rustle in the dark above caused him to glance up where he saw a pale swan gliding down the stairs, the feathers whispering on the steps, until the figure saw him and paused, the masked face still in the upper twilight.

Henry would know that figure anywhere, and he allowed himself to appreciate the flattering curves of the costume, perfectly themed for the Fairy Tale Ball. She had won the Miss Georgia Scholarship at 18 years of age, back in 2010 when there had still been a swimsuit competition.

"Isabella Thorpe," he said.

"Henry," she said. "I heard you would be here tonight." Isabella continued down the steps and stood opposite him. "It's almost midnight. Don't you have a job to do?"

"In a minute. Why would you, of all people, wear a mask? Let me see your face."

She paused for a moment and then removed the white-feathered mask – revealing red, puffy eyes and poorly salvaged makeup, still runny from tears.

"Izzy," Henry said in a low tone. "I'm sorry. Is it too soon for you to be here after your husband...?"

Her eyes swam with tears again at such unexpected sympathy, and she looked panicked for a moment, having nothing to stop them.

Henry fished a handkerchief out of his jacket pocket. "Here," he said. "I sweat a lot when I perform." He winced and said, "I mean, it's not sweaty yet. It's clean. I haven't used it yet." He exhaled and wondered how he could be a master of improvisation on stage and completely unravel with an audience of one. This one. He tried again. "Why are you crying? Can I do anything for you?" This was where having a sister came in handy.

She blotted her face and said in a deep Southern drawl, "*I have always depended upon the kindness of strangers,*" imitating Blanche DuBois, a role she had played opposite his Stanley Kowalski in high school.

"Because the cruelty of friends hurts too much," she said in her own voice.

"OK, I don't like the *Streetcar Named Desire* reference. I am not Stanley Kowalski in this situation. Do you remember how traumatic it was to practice the scene before the off-stage rape? We were in high school! What were we doing performing that play? That is not a good memory. How about *The Lion, the Witch and the Wardrobe* instead? You made a beautiful Susan."

"And you were my brother Peter."

"Yeah... I was never able to muster brotherly feelings for you, which is why I thought of it just now."

"It's just all so meaningless, Henry," she said, tearing up again.

"Theater? I don't know – it's had a role historically in changing culture. Look at –"

"No, Christmas! Christmas is so meaningless!"

"Oh! Christmas! OK." He took a second to change gears. "That's something I always loved about you, Izzy. There's really no small talk – you just dive right into the deep end. 'Christmas is meaningless.'"

She sniffed. "All the Christmas movies tell you it's about family and friends and... and being together and finding love. But what if your family is dysfunctional?" She looked up at him and remembered the loss of both his parents in high school. "And what if your parents are gone?" she said.

This is not the right time to tell her that I've loved her for twenty years, Henry said to himself as he tried to focus on her crisis.

"And what if you have no friends – because no one who you want to be friends with likes you back? And what if you've been married three times and... and... no one has ever really loved you?" A tear coursed down her face, and she made further use of Henry's handkerchief, blackening it with mascara.

Henry wondered when he could hold her without it being weird, or taking advantage, or breaking the feathers.

"And then everybody agrees, all at once at Christmas, to celebrate some promise of hope – and then nothing happens!" She spread her arms wide to expose the fakery. "And it's over at midnight on December 25th! Moving on to the New Year! – and to New Year's resolutions and another round of meaningless holidays! What are we even celebrating?" Her voice echoed in the stairwell and choked on a sob.

Henry pondered her words as his eyes traveled over the magnificent costume she wore, completely constructed of white feathers, arranged in a swirl around her hips, layered around her bosom – and he unexpectedly thought of his son's mother, Maria Bertram. Not that Izzy reminded him of Maria – but that on Christmas Eve, Maria had told him something she'd learned at her church about Christmas. Something that applied here. Something about swans.

He quickly counted the dates on his fingers and said, "Izzy, there *is* meaning. I just heard about this last week, and you'll love it – Christmas doesn't end on the 25th. Christmas Day is only the First Day of Christmas. Today,

December 31st, is the Seventh Day of Christmas." He started humming *The Twelve Days of Christmas*.

Izzy sniffed. "So, what is today? Seven Maids a-Milking?"

"No," Henry said. "Seven Swans a-Swimming."

Izzy looked up at him in surprise.

"And it's not just an annoying, repetitive song. The seven swans represent something important. My friend said that the number stands for... the seven gifts of the Holy Spirit... which are different from the Fruits of the Spirit, and I'm not sure why... and I don't remember what the gifts are, but they're something about compassion and encouragement... I dunno – but they're good, and they're gifts that last all year round."

"And what do the swans mean?" Izzy asked, suspicious of what he was selling.

"Grace. And Beauty. Gifts that are already yours. And the water the swans are swimming in stands for... cleansing. Renewal. Like – like living water, my friend said, or... or love that never runs out. And –" Here, Henry relied upon his improvisational skills. "It's important that you are dressed as a swan today. Because all of this meaning... is for you."

"But I didn't know that today was 'seven swans a-swimming!'"

"No, you didn't. But then – the meaning of Christmas doesn't come from us."

Izzy had no answer for that and considered in silence.

As Henry watched her, he asked himself, *Who could befriend this woman?* Would his sister Mary finally be mature enough more than a decade after high school to be kind to a prettier woman? His childhood friend, mother of his son, returned to mind. She had just done the unthinkable by including him in her family's Christmas Eve celebration, allowing him to have a relationship with his son, forgiving him for his part in her rewritten life. If she could do all that, she wouldn't judge Isabella Thorpe. Maria Bertram might be the perfect friend for Izzy.

The door to the stairwell opened and a head poked inside. "Oh, thank *God*!" the staff member said. "Mr. Crawford, I've been looking for you *everywhere*! There's literally *two minutes* until the countdown. You've *got* to get out there!"

"Thank you! I'll be right there. Please give me a moment," Henry said.

The staffer stared at him and said, "No, really. It's like a minute-and-a-half now."

"You go now, and I will be there for the countdown. Thank you," Henry said firmly.

The staffer withdrew his head, nostrils flared.

"Izzy," Henry said quickly, "Would you come to dinner with me next week to meet an old friend of mine and her fiancé? I just met him on Christmas Eve. They are... remarkable people, and I know they would love to meet you. I think you'd like them, too. Real friends are hard to come by – and I think she's... real-friend material."

"Weren't you with the Bertrams on Christmas Eve?"

Henry felt caught, though he wasn't sure why.

"I follow your sister's Instagram feed," she said in response to his frozen expression.

"Yes, I got to spend Christmas Eve with our oldest friends – and my son," he added.

"I assume you're referring to Maria Bertram. Is she the one who told you all this about the swans and Christmas?"

Again, Henry sensed deep waters he could not yet fathom. "Yes, I am. She is."

"Let me make sure I understand: did you just invite me on a double date with the mother of your love-child?" she asked.

Henry paused, plumbing the depth of the problem and considering the potential dangers of that friendship.

"Yes," he said.

Izzy folded the handkerchief and handed it back to him.

"Thank you, Henry," she said. "I'd love to come."

How could the Eternal do a temporal act,
The Infinite become a finite fact?
Nothing can save us that is possible:
We who must die demand a miracle.
— W. H. Auden

About the Author

Kate Susong studied English literature and theater at Princeton, exploring the history of storytelling and performing literature on stage. She moved to New York City where she acted with the Prospect Theater Company and earned a graduate degree in English and comparative literature from Columbia. After moving home to Atlanta, she produced the opera *Little Women*, began writing and performing for local schools, and wrote for the children's television show *Wondermore*, in which she also acted. She has written a novel based on *Jane Eyre* and now writes monthly essays and stories on her Substack, katesusong.com. She and her husband Kirk attend Christchurch Presbyterian in Atlanta and have two children who are their delight.

ABOUT REVERTED PRESS

"Reverted" means to return to a previous state. It comes from the Latin *revertere*. In his 4th century Latin translation of the Bible, Jerome used *revertere* dozens of times – it's a common concept, after all – but never more powerfully than when exhorting us to "return to God."

Returning to God implies that we started with him in the first place – and, in fact, that's what the whole Bible is about: a return to peace, wholeness, and relationship with God. We had it in Eden; we lost it when we preferred our own way; and even though we hate our suffering and brokenness – we still want our own way. We want to have our poison and eat it, too.

But our Creator loves us – so he ate the poison and gave us cake. Put another way, he drank the cup of wrath so we could drink the cup of blessing. He reversed the inevitability of Death by dying and returning to Life.

That reversal is the true story that is echoed in all happy endings printed by Reverted Press.

I have blotted out your transgressions like a cloud and your sins like mist; return to me, for I have redeemed you.
Isaiah 44:22